BRIDGE
1/13/2151 1704 HOURS

"Captain Archer," Roan said without preamble. "I have been instructed to read you the following statement. *Enterprise*, your presence in Sarkassian territory is an act of aggression, which we take as indication that hostilities exist between our two peoples. Should you wish to provide an explanation for your presence, it must be given according to the protocols of Contact between the Empire and outside races. Only ministerial-level officials may preside over such contact. Do you wish to provide such an explanation?"

"I've already told you—"

"Captain, do you wish to provide such an explanation to the appropriate government official?"

Reed saw the captain visibly holding his temper. At that second, his display beeped, and he looked down and saw something else.

The two Sarkassian ships had charged their weapons systems.

ENTERPRISE™

WHAT PRICE HONOR?

DAVE STERN

Based on *Star Trek*®
created by Gene Roddenberry
Based on *Enterprise*™
created by Rick Berman & Brannon Braga

POCKET BOOKS

New York   London   Toronto   Sydney   Singapore

This book is a work of fiction. Names, characters, places and incidents are products of the author's imagination or are used fictitiously. Any resemblance to actual events or locales or persons, living or dead, is entirely coincidental.

An *Original* Publication of POCKET BOOKS

POCKET BOOKS, a division of Simon & Schuster, Inc.
1230 Avenue of the Americas, New York, NY 10020

Copyright © 2002 by Paramount Pictures. All Rights Reserved.

STAR TREK is a Registered Trademark of Paramount Pictures.

This book is published by Pocket Books, a division of Simon & Schuster, Inc., under exclusive license from Paramount Pictures.

ISBN: 0-7434-6278-5

First Pocket Books printing November 2002

10 9 8 7 6 5 4 3 2 1

POCKET and colophon are registered trademarks of Simon & Schuster, Inc.

For information regarding special discounts for bulk purchases, please contact Simon & Schuster Special Sales at 1-800-456-6798 or business@simonandschuster.com

Printed in the U.S.A.

To Dr. Bones, Ollie Jones, Tree Tavern Pizza,
the real WPIX,
Tiny, Steiny, Bet, and Larry. . . .

Six o'clock it is, was, and forever will be.

Prologue

STARS DRIFTED BY. The impulse reactor thrummed.

Alone in his ready room, Jonathan Archer tapped his fingers on his desk. He shifted in his seat, and frowned. He opened his mouth to speak, paused, then shook his head and stood up. He paced the length of the small room once, twice, a third time, instinctually ducking the bulkheads.

"Damn," he said, and sat back down at his workstation.

There was no easy way to say this. Might as well just get started.

He keyed a series of commands into his computer. It chirped at him. He cleared his throat, and started speaking.

"Message begins," he said. "Captain Jonathan Archer of the *Starship Enterprise* to Nicole and Jonathan Hart, Lake Armstrong. Mr. and Ms.

Hart, on behalf of all Starfleet, and most particularly the armory crew of the *Enterprise* . . ."

Archer's voice trailed off. He frowned.

"No. That's not right," he said, and keyed in the erase command. Third time he'd started the message; third time he'd deleted it. It wasn't like him to be indecisive like this—or indecisive about anything, in fact. That wasn't how he'd gotten to be captain of the fastest ship in the fleet. How he'd gotten to be the man leading Starfleet out into the galaxy.

He looked at the monitor before him. In the dim light of the ready room, he saw his own face reflected on the display screen. A hazy shadow, an imprecise rendering of the man he was. The imprecision hid the lines on his face, the flecks of gray at his temples, and for a moment Archer imagined himself as he was without them twenty years ago, a young man, with no responsibilities, with an endless sea of possibilities ahead of him. He had drifted for a while in those early years, angry about the patronizing treatment humankind had received from its reluctant tutors, the Vulcans, angry about a career in Starfleet that seemed unlikely to ever lead him out into the stars, angry in particular for how his father had been cheated of his lifelong desire. But he'd found his way past the anger, found a way to channel his emotions into a productive career.

Some people never got that chance.

Archer shifted in his chair, and his reflection vanished from the screen. The display came into focus. It was split into three sections—a horizontal bar of text at the bottom, with two boxes stacked, one next to the other, above it. The box on the right was all text. The box on the left contained a young woman's picture—a standard Starfleet ID photo. He quickly scanned the text to the right of it.

Alana Marie Hart
DOB: 4.4.2125
POB: Lake Armstrong, Luna
Graduated: Perth University 2146 *cum laude*
Rank: Ensign
Serial #: SC 007–8787
Enlisted Starfleet 2146

Hart had jet black hair, a round face, and a hard set to her jaw. The expression distorted her features—pulled her brow down, scrunched up her nose, thinned her lips. Archer remembered the first time he'd seen her picture, thinking immediately that she'd be much more attractive in person. He'd been right.

They'd met on *Enterprise*'s third day out from Kronos, after delivering Klaang back to his people, after Admiral Forrest had given Archer the go-ahead to continue the ship's mission. The captain had set up meetings with every member of the crew—ten minutes or so, just to get to know the faces aboard his ship. Most of the meetings had gone on longer than that.

Not Ensign Hart's.

She'd entered his ready room at attention, her gaze fixed not on Archer but the wall behind him, wearing the same grimly determined look on her face.

"At ease, Ensign," Archer said.

Hart was tall, and angular. She snapped into position, her hands behind her back, her elbows jutting out to her sides like weapons.

"Yes, sir!"

"I meant relax," he said. "Smile, if you like."

She looked directly at him for the first time. "Sir?" she asked, a puzzled look spreading across her features. For a second then, the frown disappeared, her face and features relaxed, and the captain saw that he'd guessed right.

Ensign Hart was beautiful.

He grinned at her. "I said smile. Like this."

"Yes, sir!" The edges of her mouth went up reflexively, and then snapped right back down, like a door sliding shut.

She looked toward him expectantly.

"Very good," Archer said a second later, and then went on with the interview, which was similarly unrevealing. Questions from him, clipped answers ("Yes, sir," and "No, sir") from her. Archer cut it short after two minutes. He'd always meant to set up another meeting with her after a few months went by, after she'd had a chance to get comfortable aboard the ship. But he'd never been able to find the time.

Archer turned his attention back to the monitor. The display—a single line of text scrolling across the screen like an old-fashioned news ticker, displaying (among other things) the date, *Enterprise*'s coordinates, systems status, and ship's time. It was 1415. He'd been in the ready room for twenty minutes—long enough to send a dozen messages to Hart's parents.

He was stalling. Hoping that inspiration would strike, that he would find exactly the right thing to say. Except that there was no right thing to say in a situation like this.

The com beeped. Archer pressed a switch on the panel.

"Captain?" It was Hoshi, in communications.

"Go ahead."

"The Sarkassian ship is hailing us. They're requesting permission to dock."

"They're here already?" Stupid question, and he knew it the minute he spoke.

"Yes, sir."

"Damn," Archer said under his breath. He had to be there to greet the ambassador. Relations between the two races had gotten off to a rocky start, and Archer couldn't afford to do anything that might make things worse.

"Captain? Ambassador Valay sounds pretty insistent, sir."

Archer could believe that. She hadn't struck him as the patient type. "All right. Send them to launch bay two. I'm on my way. And I'll want you with me when they dock. Archer out."

He turned off the com, and turned back to the monitor. As he did so, the last few lines of Ensign Hart's service record caught his eye.

Posted Europa Base 6/2/46
Achilles 2/8/49
Promoted to Ensign 11/11/50
Assigned Enterprise 1/30/51
Deceased: 1/14/52

The captain sighed. He should send Hart's parents a simple message of condolence. Speak plainly, which Archer always prided himself on doing. Except plain speaking in this instance came off as cold and insensitive. Plain speaking in this instance went something like: *Folks, your daughter's dead. She went crazy, and one of my officers had to shoot her.*

No. He had to say something beyond that.

Except it would have to be later. For now, the Sarkassians were here, and he had to focus on finding a way to smooth over relations with them.

He stood up then, clearing Hart's picture and record from the screen, and exited the ready room.

One

LIEUTENANT MALCOLM REED turned the metal fragment over in his hands, brushing away some of the dirt clinging to it as he did so. It was roughly the size and shape of a brick, a thick, dull gray-colored mass that he'd fully expected would weigh about the same as titanium. When he picked it up, though, he was surprised to discover it was significantly less heavy—literally as light as a feather. An unusual alloy, one that had already proven resistant—in fact, impervious—to the usual battery of scans.

Scattered on the table in front of him were a dozen or so metal fragments identical to the one in his hand—debris the landing party had brought back from the ruins of the Sarkassian outpost to analyze. Standing behind him were

Crewmen Duel and Perkins, whom the captain had assigned to help him.

Normally this kind of scientific analysis would have been out of Reed's field of expertise. But Captain Archer had agreed with him that a different approach to analyzing the material—an approach that focused on determining what sort of weapons could have destroyed it—might prove helpful. And that kind of analysis, Reed could handle.

Except now, Reed wondered if the captain had been humoring him.

Everyone had handled him with kid gloves all day—Trip ("Maybe you should take some time"), Dr. Phlox ("If you want to talk, my schedule is wide open"), even Hoshi ("I'm around if you need me"), they all treated him like he might go to pieces at any second. Well, that wasn't going to happen. He was fine. Tired, but fine.

"Sir?"

He looked up and saw Perkins staring at him.

"Did you say something?"

"Did I say something?" Had he spoken aloud? Reed shook his head. "No. I most certainly did not."

"Yes, sir," Perkins said, with a look of sympathy on his face. "Sorry, sir."

Reed almost snapped at him. Then he remembered that with Hart gone, there was a vacancy in the armory rotation. He also remembered that Perkins had put in for a transfer to weapons duty some time ago, and so Reed would more than likely be working very closely with him for the foreseeable future. There was no sense in getting off on the wrong foot with the man.

So instead of snapping, Reed took a deep breath, and turned back to the fragment.

"All right, let's get started."

"What's up first, sir?" Duel asked.

"A stress test, I would think," Perkins said instantly. "Even if we can't directly scan the material, we can infer a number of things from its behavior under various conditions. Wouldn't you agree, sir?"

The two looked toward Reed expectantly. Reed looked back at them. Duel was short and squat, Perkins tall and thin. An old nursery rhyme floated through his mind, and he smiled. Only for a moment.

This was not an occasion for levity.

"No. I'd prefer to start with a spectrographic analysis of this dust. Perhaps it can provide us with some clues." Reed brushed off another chunk of caked-on dirt from the fragment. "We might be able to pick up traces of whatever material . . ." His voice trailed off.

"Sir?" Perkins prompted.

"Hang on a minute." Reed ran his fingers along the fragment. Clearing away the debris had exposed a raised surface on one side of it—a design of some sort?

He laid the fragment down on the table so that the raised surface was facing up. Then he began clearing away dust from some of the other fragments. Behind him, he sensed Duel and Perkins crowding closer.

Fully half the fragments had the same sort of ridges on the back.

"Are those more symbols?" he heard one of them ask.

"Yes," Reed said, nodding. "Indeed they are." They looked, in fact, identical to the ones they'd found throughout the outpost. Symbols, though, were not his field of expertise.

He walked over to the com panel, and opened a channel.

"Reed to bridge."

"Bridge. T'Pol here."

"Can I speak to Hoshi, Sub-Commander?"

"No."

"No?"

"No. She and the captain are in launch bay two, greeting the Sarkassian ambassador."

Reed's mouth almost fell open.

"The Sarkassians are here?"

"That is what I just said."

Reed nodded grimly. He would have expected to meet with the Sarkassians as well. He should be there—a potentially hostile race coming aboard *Enterprise*. Mentally, he added the captain to the list of those treating him with kid gloves.

"We've found some more symbols—on the fragments in the science lab," Reed said to T'Pol. "She should know about this."

"She is occupied right now," T'Pol told him.

"But—"

"Is this an emergency?"

"No."

"Then it will have to wait. T'Pol out."

Reed stared at the com panel a second. It wasn't an emergency. But Hoshi would likely be with the captain, and the Sarkassians, for the rest of the day. At least several more hours.

This might be a clue. And Reed couldn't wait that long to find out.

"I'm going to launch bay two." He cleared his throat. "I'll be back shortly. In the meantime, I'd like a full spectrographic analysis. You can run your stress test too, Mister Perkins—only not on any of the fragments with symbols. I want Hoshi to see these just as they are."

Perkins nodded. "Yes, sir."

"Of course, sir," Duel said.

"Carry on then," Reed said, and set off at a brisk walk toward the nearest turbolift.

When he arrived at launch bay two, Captain Archer and Hoshi were standing on the main deck, facing the Sarkassian ambassador and two others of her race.

The Sarkassians were humanoid, and as pale

and thin in person as they'd appeared on the viewscreen. They looked anemic to him, as if they'd spent their entire life indoors. Perhaps they had—they clearly had no aversion to enclosed spaces, as the ambassador's shuttle, like the larger ship that had first contacted *Enterprise*, was windowless, a seamless surface of shining black metal.

"We want to accommodate you," Captain Archer was saying. "But—"

"Good," the ambassador interrupted. Her voice had a harsh, grating quality that hadn't been clear over the com system. "Then you will turn the prisoner over to us."

Ambassador Valay stood front and center in her party. She wore a long, iridescent purple robe that shimmered in the bright glare of the overhead lights. Her long red hair was held back from her face by an elaborate silver headpiece, more of a crown almost, with three sparkling red gems set in its face. Each stone was about the size of an egg—by Earth standards, Valay was wearing a fortune in jewels on her head. Whether or not Sarkassians valued such things the same way humans did was an open question, but at any rate, the headpiece made for an impressive display.

Reed was not as taken with the woman wearing it.

"I grow tired of having to repeat myself, Captain," Valay said.

"Forgive me, Ambassador," Archer said. "I'm afraid turning the prisoner over to you is not as simple a question as you make it out to be."

"It is precisely that simple, Captain," Valay said. "Our war is none of your concern."

"It is now," Archer said. "One of my crew is dead, and I'd like the chance to question this man about that."

"You have my sympathies, Captain," Valay interrupted, though her tone of voice suggested anything but compassion. She shook a long, thin finger at Archer. "But let me put the matter in perspective for you. You have one dead crewman. There were close to sixty people working in the facility below us, and every single one of them is now a body for me to bring back to their families. You are holding the person responsible for that outrage, and I want him."

"You may see him," Archer said. "But until I know exactly what went on down there—"

"Have you not heard what I've said? This man is responsible—for your crewman's death, the death of our scientists, everything. There is no doubt."

"There is in my mind," Archer said. "The pictures you transmitted to us are not an exact likeness. Moreover—"

"He has most assuredly been using drugs to alter the pigmentation of his skin," said the third member of the Sarkassian party. "Which is no doubt how he got onto the outpost in the first place."

"I will provide you evidence, Captain," the ambassador said. "He has used similar methods in the past. This man is a murderer many times over, a butcher, a—" The translator spluttered in a burst of static.

"I'm sorry. Could you say that again?" Hoshi said, stepping forward and holding the translator out in front of her.

The ambassador repeated the phrase and—as before—the translator spluttered.

Valay turned away, exasperated.

"We are wasting time!"

Hoshi exchanged a frustrated glance with Archer. At that instant, the captain caught sight of Reed.

"Excuse me, Captain," Reed said, taking a step forward. "If you can spare a minute."

Everyone on deck—including the Sarkassians—turned his way.

"This is Lieutenant Reed," Archer said, motioning him closer. "Our armory officer. Lieutenant, this is Ambassador Valay."

Reed inclined his head in greeting. The ambassador did the same.

"Lieutenant," she said. "May I present Commodore Roan, and Dr. Natir."

Reed nodded to each of them. They, in turn, bowed back. Both wore robes similar to Valay's, though of different colors—Natir's a lighter purple than Valay's, Roan's a simple black. Natir was the man who had accused the prisoner of deliberately changing the pigmentation of his skin. And now that Reed was closer, he recognized Roan from their first contact with the Sarkassians. The commodore was older than Valay, his skin even paler than hers, save for a mottled patch of red and brown running all the way down one side of his face and neck. It looked like a very bad burn.

"Armory officer," Roan said, nodding to himself. "I guessed right, then."

"Sir?"

"The other day, when we first made contact? Before the translators were working?"

"I remember," Reed said, images from those chaotic moments—rushing back from the planet's surface, Phlox working on Ensign Hart, the few brief glimpses he'd had of the Sarkassian ship's interior—flashing through his mind.

"I had my communications officer maintain visual contact with your ship. Which offered me a chance to see you all at work."

"And in those few moments, you managed to pick me out as the armory officer?"

"I recognize the type," Roan said. "Having been one myself for quite a long time."

"Really?"

"Yes, really."

"I'd be interested to know what gave me away."

"Perhaps if we have a few moments later, I can tell you."

"I would like that," Reed said.

"And I would like to get back to the business at hand," Valay interrupted.

Roan turned and bowed to her. "Forgive me, Ambassador."

"Your efforts at establishing relations are appreciated, Commodore," Valay said, in a tone of voice that suggested just the opposite. "Please bear in mind, however, our primary duty is to those who perished on the outpost below."

"Of course," Roan said, tight-lipped.

Reed looked from one of them to the other, puzzled. He sensed a lot of hostility bubbling underneath the surface of their polite conversation, and wondered where it all came from. He caught the captain's eye, and knew Archer was wondering the same thing.

"Though I am curious, Captain," Valay continued, turning her attention to Archer again. "Your earlier statements led me to believe that *Enterprise* was primarily an exploratory vessel, not a warship."

"We use our weapons in self-defense only," Archer said.

"As do we," Valay said. "All civilized species recognize self-defense as their fundamental right. Which is why you must allow us to take custody of this prisoner. He has committed multiple acts of war against my people!"

Archer smiled tightly. Reed rarely saw that smile. In his experience, it usually preceded one of the captain's very infrequent outbursts of temper.

"Excuse me a moment, will you, Ambassador?" Archer put his hand on Reed's arm. "We'll be right back."

The captain pulled Reed off to the far side of the shuttlebay.

"Not that I don't appreciate the interruption—but if I had wanted you to be here, Malcolm . . ."

"I'm sorry, sir, but we've found something." Reed told the captain about the symbols. "I thought Hoshi would want to see them—see if they—"

"I can't spare her right now," Archer interrupted. "The situation here is too delicate. Carstairs has been doing a lot of the work on what we found down there. Use him." The captain looked back toward the ambassador and her party. "If that's all—"

"Yes, sir." Reed tried not to let his disappointment show. "I'll be back in the armory then—if you need me."

As he turned to go, Archer put a hand on his shoulder.

"Malcolm, wait."

Reed spun back around to see the captain looking at him with concern. "Did you get any sleep at all?"

"A little. I think."

"You think?"

Reed shrugged. "Maybe. I don't know."

In fact, he was pretty sure that he hadn't, that the few dreamlike hours he'd spent lying in his bunk had been just that—dreamlike, not actual sleep at all. But he didn't need rest—that could come later.

What he needed now were answers.

"We're going to find out what happened. I give you my word," Archer said, as if reading his mind. "Why don't you take the rest of today off, let Trip and Lieutenant Hess cover the armory—"

"Not necessary, sir."

"Malcolm, there's only so much you can do."

Reed nodded. The captain was right about that. In fact, right now there was absolutely nothing for him to do—except wait.

Which, given his state of mind, was simply unacceptable.

He glanced back toward the ambassador and the other Sarkassians, and an idea popped into his head.

"Captain," he began. "Forgive me for speaking plainly, but Ambassador Valay—is she as difficult to talk to as she seems?"

"More so," Archer said. "But she's who we've got to deal with."

"That *you* have to deal with."

Archer eyed him curiously. "Malcolm?"

"I might be able to speak more freely to Commodore Roan."

"I take it you're volunteering to accompany us."

"Yes, sir."

The captain frowned. "I don't know. This is a first contact. A very delicate one. I don't want Starfleet to be speaking with two different voices to the Sarkassians."

"The point is for him to talk, sir. Not me."

Archer thought for a moment. "All right," he said finally. "Why don't you join us, and see what you can find out about that outpost."

"Yes, sir. I'll try and find out more about the prisoner as well. This—" Reed struggled to remember his name.

"Goridian."

"Goridian. Yes." Reed hesitated. "Are you going to let the ambassador take him?"

"Eventually, I suppose. But not before I find out what was going on down there. If it had something to do with what happened to Ensign Hart."

"Yes, sir," Reed said. His voice took on an edge. "Hard to see how it couldn't have."

"I agree." The captain put a hand on Reed's shoulder. "No one blames you, Malcolm."

"I know that," Reed said.

But his hands were fists. His heart was hammering. He blamed himself.

All night long, that was all he'd been doing. Thinking about the past, about what he'd done, and what he hadn't. Thinking about Alana, her voice so clear and vivid in his head it was as if she were right there with him, as if the past had suddenly come back to life.

His vision blurred for a second, and he remembered.

Two

CORRIDOR, E-DECK
12/31/2150 2127 HOURS

IT WAS NEW YEAR'S EVE, and Reed was on his way
from one party to another. Holding a champagne
glass in his left hand, as he studied the padd in his
right. Lieutenant Hess in engineering had a relative who worked in one of the vineyards in the
Champagne region. She'd arranged to have a mag-
num brought aboard, and Reed intended to savor
every drop. He wasn't sure how good the bubbly
would be at the captain's party later that evening.

He glanced down at the padd as he walked, not-
ing with satisfaction that he'd taken care of almost everything on his list today, and the things
that he hadn't done could all wait until—

He stopped short.

"Oh, damn," he said, looking at the last item on
his list, which read "TB1 FR Time?" How he'd for-

gotten about it all day was beyond him. TB1 was torpedo bay one, and FR was fire response, and the note was meant to remind him that there was a problem with bay one's launch mechanism. Fire-response time was up by almost five percent, and every nanosecond in a combat situation was critical.

Earlier in the day he'd asked Ensign Santini, who had pulled the duty shift in the armory tonight, to check the firing relays for mechanical defects, though the lieutenant suspected the problem was in software, not hardware. Whatever it was, Reed was certain it wouldn't take him long to find and fix, and then it would be off to his quarters, and then the captain's mess, and a Happy New Year to one and all.

He took the turbolift down to F-deck, then headed toward the armory. The door slid open, Reed walked in, and to his surprise he saw not Santini but Ensign Hart—Alana Hart—on duty. She stood next to a monitor in the back of the room, studying something on the screen. Reed couldn't tell what from where he stood.

He took the opportunity to study her for a moment.

Hart was something of an enigma to him— they'd served together for a year now, and in all that time, he couldn't recall exchanging more than two dozen words with her. Every attempt at a conversation he'd made had been—well, *rebuffed* was the wrong word, because she'd answered his questions (if "Yes, sir" and "No, sir" and "It was fine, sir" counted as answers)—tolerated, and not much more. He was her superior officer, so it never got close to rudeness with him, but he'd heard rumblings from some of the other crew about a certain . . . prickliness to her manner.

At first, Reed thought it was just her way of coping with a new situation. Especially after coming over from the *Achilles*, she was bound to be both closemouthed and a little defensive— about herself, and about the past. Add into the mix the fact that Hart was an attractive woman ("easy on the eyes" was how Diaz had put it, and Reed couldn't dispute that, though of course with him being her superior any sort of romance between them was forbidden by regulations) and Reed thought he had a handle on the reasons for her behavior. So he hadn't made an issue of it, thinking that time would mellow her.

But he'd been wrong. Nearly a year into the mission, and she showed no signs of coming out of her shell.

Now, perhaps, was a chance for him to address the issue.

Except, he considered, that it was New Year's Eve, and the middle of the armory didn't necessarily strike him as the appropriate place for a private conversation. Some point over the next few days, though—for certain.

"Ensign," he said, clearing his throat.

Hart spun around, surprise on her face. "Sir."

She stood ramrod-straight, eyes front, not moving a muscle, as if Reed were about to give her and her uniform a thorough inspection.

"At ease," Reed said. "Relax."

"Yes, sir." She clasped her hands behind her back and shifted position, relaxing not a single inch. Reed sighed. Another thing about Hart—she was a stickler for regulations. True, Starfleet was a military organization, and Reed, coming from a long line of naval officers, appreciated the tradition as much as anyone, but . . .

It was New Year's Eve, for pity's sake.

"What are you doing here?"

"Ensign Santini asked me to check on the firing mechanism, sir."

"That's not what I meant," Reed said. "Where is Ensign Santini?"

"Oh. I took his shift. He wanted to go to the engineering party."

"Ah." Reed nodded. "That was very considerate of you, Ensign. I hope Mister Santini will return the favor at some point."

"Yes, sir," she said, in such a way that Reed got the impression that it didn't matter to her one bit if Santini reciprocated or not.

"Did he talk to you about the firing-response lag in bay one?"

"Yes, sir," she said, crossing quickly to the starboard launch tube. "I was able to find the problem, I believe."

"Really?" Reed asked.

"Yes, sir. Come see here." She crossed to the starboard launch tube, and crouched down next to it, flashlight in hand. Reed came around the far side of the tube, setting his padd and the glass of champagne down on the firing console behind the bay, and crouched down across from her. She'd opened up the inside access panel. A tangle of cable and logic boards lay spread out across the bottom of the tube, next to the firing mechanism.

"Well, first I thought that it couldn't be a mechanical problem. I thought the problem was in software, since we've made so many modifications to the basic system since we left spacedock."

Reed nodded. "My thinking exactly."

"But I was wrong," she said.

"Really?"

"Yes." She pointed the flashlight into the empty bay. "Look there."

Reed looked where the light was pointing, and saw immediately what she meant. A half-meter length of cable—one of the power conduits, Reed guessed, judging from its thickness—lay curled up next to the side of the bay. One side of it was burned black.

"Good lord," he said. "How did we miss that?"

"It looks worse than it is," Hart said. "Electron

flow is only inhibited point zero five percent in the circuit."

"Hang the electron flow. A cable in that condition could have done same serious damage down the road. Good work, Ensign. Above and beyond," Reed said.

"Yes, sir," Hart said. "Thank you, sir."

Reed braced his hand on the console behind him, stood up—

And knocked over his glass of champagne. He watched it tumble, as if in slow motion, and spill into the torpedo bay, splashing all over the exposed wiring. Sparks fizzled. He heard a crackling sound.

He reached for the emergency shutdown switch underneath the console—and brushed against Hart's hand as she got there first, and pulled it.

The room promptly went dark, except for the emergency lights.

Reed stood stock-still for a split second.

"That was the single stupidest thing I've ever done in my life," he said finally.

"It was an accident, sir," Hart said. "Accidents happen."

"Not to me they don't. Damn stupid. Totally against protocol, bringing that champagne in here." Reed sighed. "All right. Let's see how bad the damage is."

He crossed to the back of the room and accessed the emergency panel. He brought the overhead lights back online. Hart, he saw, already had her tools out and was pulling the rest of the bay's access panel off.

"It's all right, Ensign," he called. "You don't have to help with that. It's my fault. I'll handle the cleanup."

"Partially my fault too, sir. I distracted you. If you hadn't stopped to see what I was doing . . ."

"That's stretching it a bit, but . . . all right. I appreciate the help. Thank you."

He started back across the room. Halfway there, the com sounded.

"Bridge to armory. Weapons systems just went offline. Report."

That was T'Pol. Reed went to the com.

"Reed here, Sub-Commander. We've had an accident. Nothing serious."

"Very well. When do you estimate having weapons back online?"

Reed looked over at Hart, who was scanning the interior of the bay with a flashlight. She shrugged at his unspoken question.

"Not long," Reed said. "Will advise."

"Very well. Bridge out."

Reed shut the com, and came the rest of the way across the room. "How bad does it look? Can you—"

The com sounded again.

"Engineering to armory. Primary weapons systems are offline, do you copy? Over."

Reed sighed, and turned around again.

"I copy. This is Lieutenant Reed in the armory. We've had an accident. I'll keep you posted on our progress. Out."

He looked back across the room at Hart. "Maybe I should just stand here until everyone aboard checks in."

"If you think best, sir," Hart replied, without looking up.

"Ah—that was a joke, Ensign."

"Yes, sir," she said, and went right on working.

Reed sighed, and went to get the diagnostic kit from the back of the armory. On his way, he passed the monitor Hart had been looking at when he came in.

There was a picture up on the screen—a man in his forties, with a long, thin face and a shock of short gray hair. Reed stopped and studied it a moment.

The man looked oddly familiar to him.

"Who's this, Ensign?" He turned around just as Hart was looking up from the console.

The expression on her face was one of sheer horror.

"Oh. I'm sorry I left that on the display—I'll clear it right away."

"It's all right," Reed said, surprised at Hart's reaction. "I'm sorry. I didn't mean to pry, I just saw the picture and—"

Hart had kept moving while he talked, practically dashing across the armory. Now she reached the workstation, and cleared the image on it, virtually shoving him out of the way to operate the controls. Her face was flushed, almost beet red.

"Ensign, what—"

"Sorry, sir." She lowered her head. "It's personal. I would rather not talk about it."

"Of course," Reed nodded. "I apologize again for intruding."

She went back to the firing bay. He got the diagnostic kit. They worked for close to an hour to disassemble the bay and check the integrity of every circuit in it, in that whole time exchanging not a single extraneous word. More than once, Reed thought about asking about the picture and the man in it, but from the way Hart deliberately avoided eye contact with him, he decided the effort would be fruitless. He'd talk to her about it at some point, of course: he was her direct superior, and he had perhaps an opportunity here to get to know her in a way he hadn't before.

"That seems to be everything," he said as they resealed the bay's access panel. "Thank you again, Ensign."

"You're quite welcome, sir."

He shook his head again, thinking of how stupid he had been to leave his glass on the console. "I'm sorry to put you to all that unnecessary work, though I suppose it would have been worse if I'd spilled it back in engineering—could have ended up in the warp core, or the dilithium chamber, or—"

He stopped in midsentence, because all of a sudden he remembered where he'd seen the man in the picture before. Given Hart's service record, he was surprised it had taken him so long to recognize him.

"That was Captain Lyman's picture you were looking at," Reed said. "From the *Achilles.*"

"Yes, sir," Hart said, bowing her head.

"Ensign," Reed said. "Everyone knows about your service record. Everyone knows what happened to the *Achilles*, and no one holds any of that against you."

"Yes, sir," she repeated.

"So there's no reason to be ashamed of anything. No reason to hide it."

"No, sir."

Reed struggled for what to say next. The silence stretched on to an uncomfortable length.

New Year's Eve or not, it was clear he was going to have to address this issue now.

Which was, of course, when the com sounded.

"Captain Archer to Lieutenant Reed. Archer to Lieutenant Reed."

"Excuse me a moment." Reed flicked a channel open. "Right here, Captain."

He heard laughter in the background. Trip and Hoshi, it sounded like. "We're waiting on you, Malcolm."

"Yes, sir. I'll be there as quick as I can. Just finishing up with a little problem we had down here."

"Will you get out of that damn armory and get up here?" That was Trip. "All work and no play—"

"Yes, yes, I hear you," Reed said. "It really will be only a few minutes. Reed out." He closed the channel before Trip could give him any more guff, and turned back to Hart.

"I think we're all set here, sir," Hart said. "I'll get to work on repairing that cable in the firing bay, if it's all right."

Reed nodded. "Yes, of course." He hesitated a moment, then decided to press on. "Ensign—I will want to talk to you later. About Captain Lyman, and the *Achilles*."

"There's no need," she said quickly.

"It's not a request." Reed consulted his schedule. "Ten-thirty hours, day after tomorrow, in my quarters?"

Hart seemed to shrink in on herself. For a moment, then, she seemed small and tired, and very vulnerable.

"Yes, sir," she said, finally. "In your quarters, ten-thirty."

"Good." He affected a small smile. "Nice work, picking up that damaged cable. And thanks again for your help in cleaning up the champagne. Perhaps next year, we can convince you to drink some."

"Yes, sir. I'm looking forward to it."

But she didn't sound like she was.

Reed smiled again. "Happy New Year, Ensign."

"Happy New Year, sir."

He left her alone in the armory then, and headed for the captain's mess.

The whole way there, he thought about Ensign Hart.

Not good, that on a night she could have spent celebrating at any one of half a dozen parties aboard ship, she'd chosen to be by herself. Why was it so hard for her to forget the past? What had happened aboard *Achilles*?

Even as the clock chimed midnight, and the celebration in the captain's mess kicked into high gear, Reed couldn't shake the image from his mind, Hart standing before him in the armory, head bowed.

He felt sad, and sorry, and sympathetic all over again.

He felt certain that she was asking him for help.

Three

HART'S FACE FADED AWAY, and the here and now returned. Captain Archer had taken them the long way around. E-deck to the turbolift, then come all the way around C-deck to the converted crew quarters that were serving as the prisoner's cell.

At first Reed thought Archer was doing it to give himself more time to talk to the ambassador, to put their relationship on a smoother path. But the captain's attempts (a series of stop-and-start—and to Reed's eyes antagonistic—conversations) to engage her in conversation ended by the time they reached the turbolift.

As the six of them stepped out onto C-deck and proceeded down the corridor in silence, Reed began to suspect that the captain might have had a different motive altogether in choosing such a circuitous route to their destination.

Maybe Archer was giving him a chance to talk to Roan.

He fell back a step and turned to the commodore.

"So how could you tell?"

Roan looked confused for a second. Then he smiled. "How you were the ship's weapons officer? Or armory officer, if you prefer?"

"Yes—and either title is fine."

"Well," Roan fell back a step as well, "let's just say that there is a certain focus one has when one is responsible for defending so many lives. At least, if you're doing the job properly."

"Well." Reed smiled. "I'll take that as a compliment."

"You should."

"Although I have to admit a lot of my attention was focused on your ships, Commodore. They're very formidable-looking vessels."

"Yes, they are. No disputing the fact that they're designed for battle, is there?" Roan shook his head. "Part of me regrets that was your first impression of our race, Lieutenant—we are not that warlike a people. It's just that with what occurred down on the outpost . . ."

"I understand, sir." Reed decided to change the subject. "So you were a weapons officer as well?"

"Yes. But that was a long time ago. Now I command our defense forces in this sector."

"You must have had a distinguished career—for you to end up where you are now."

"Where I am now?" Roan shook his head. "Where I am now is more a matter of politics than anything else."

"Sir?"

"It's not important, Lieutenant. Let us just say that I far preferred my years aboard our Striker ships to what I do now." The commodore looked around the corridor and shook his head again. "Though I'm not sure I'm up for the rigors of extended duty at this point in my life."

"It has its drawbacks, I will admit," Reed said.

"The food?"

"No, the food here is actually quite good."

"Our food was terrible," Roan said. "Terrible. Of course, that never mattered at the time. One ate to replenish energy, not for pleasure. Back then."

"I have to admit," Reed said, "I rarely pay attention to what I'm eating."

"That's because you're still young. You have the energy to enjoy other things in life."

The two continued in silence a moment.

"I made the closest friends of my life back then," Roan said. "Aboard the *Cressoti*, and the *Brosman*—two of the ships I first served on."

"I understand completely."

35

"Your crewman who was killed," Roan said. "Did you know him?"

The question hit Reed almost like a physical blow. He forced himself to keep walking.

"Her," he said. "I did know her."

"I'm sorry." Roan stopped for a second, then looked at Reed. "Fairly well, I think—or am I wrong?"

"No. You're not."

"You served together a long time?"

"Only a year."

"A year aboard a ship like this *is* a long time. You have my sympathies, Lieutenant. It is always hard to lose a friend."

"Thank you, sir."

The two walked on. The rest of the party had gotten a good two dozen feet out in front of them, and as Reed watched, they rounded a bend in the corridor, and momentarily disappeared from sight.

"In your journeys," Roan said, "you have seen many worlds? Many civilizations?"

"Some. We're hoping that this sector will have more." And not without good reason. They were set to rendezvous with the *Shi'ar*, a Vulcan research vessel, in a few days, and that meeting marked the point where Vulcan surveys had stopped completely. From then on, *Enterprise* and her crew would largely be blazing new territory. "I don't suppose you could tell us what we might expect to find in this direction?"

"I wish I could. I wish I knew more about what is out here." Roan sounded frustrated, almost angry. "But exploration has not been a primary component of our policy for many years."

"I see." Reed paused. "What, may I ask, is the primary component of your policy?"

"Ah." Roan smiled. "You mean to say, what was the purpose of our outpost on the planetoid below?"

Reed tried to cover his surprise—then shrugged. So much for subterfuge, he thought.

"Yes," he said. "That's exactly what I mean."

"I'm afraid I'm not at liberty to answer that question, Lieutenant. At the moment."

"I understand," Reed said.

"I hope our relationship proceeds to the point where I can share that knowledge with you."

"As do I, Commodore."

Reed looked up and realized that they had arrived at the prisoner's cell.

The other four members of their party—the captain, Hoshi, Valay, and Natir—were stopped in front of it. Bishop and Crewman Diaz were there as well, on guard.

Also there—to Reed's surprise—was Dr. Phlox. He was in the middle of an argument with Dr. Natir.

"I concede your credentials in treating this species, sir," Phlox was saying. "I do not concede that my obligation to treat him ends with your arrival."

"I will be happy to let you take a sample of the serum," Natir responded. "You will see that it is harmless—it simply relaxes certain inhibitions the patient may have so that he responds more freely to questioning."

"As I mentioned before," Phlox said, a shade of irritation creeping into his voice, "the prisoner has just regained consciousness. I do not think it wise to subject him to any sort of sustained interrogation. A few questions, at most. Then he should rest."

"He is a prisoner of war," Valay said. "He does not warrant such consideration."

"He's going to get it," Archer said. "As long as he's on my ship. You may speak to him briefly. Then I will speak to him briefly. And then we will leave. I hope I make myself clear."

Valay's face darkened in anger. Which—with a very visible effort—she held in check.

"Your ship, your rules," she said finally.

"Good." Archer nodded to Bishop and Diaz, who overrode the door lock. It hissed open, and the captain stepped inside. The others followed.

When Reed moved to join them, Phlox stepped in his way.

"Lieutenant," the doctor said quietly. "I wanted you to know—the autopsy is almost done."

"And?" Reed asked. "Anything out of the ordinary?"

"Not so far. I should have final results in another hour." He looked past Reed, and into the prisoner's quarters. "I don't trust these Sarkassians at all. Excuse me."

He pushed past Reed and into the cell.

The lieutenant hesitated a moment before following him in.

Somewhere inside, Reed realized, he was suddenly nervous. He thought a moment, and decided that it must be because he associated the prisoner, Goridian, with Alana. Seeing him, Reed would be reminded of her.

But he didn't know why that should be a cause for concern. Perhaps the captain had been right—perhaps he wasn't up to this right now. He certainly hadn't been able to get anything useful out of Commodore Roan.

"Sir?"

Bishop had spoken. Reed turned to him.

"The doctor's talking about Ensign Hart?"

"Yes." The captain had insisted on an immediate autopsy, to discover if there was anything physically wrong with her that could account for her actions.

"Could you—"

"You'll know the second I do, Crewman."

"Thank you, sir."

Reed looked into the man's eyes then, and saw

genuine concern there. Which made him aware he'd been derelict in talking to the rest of the armory crew about Hart. Not so much in giving them the facts about what had happened to her, how she'd died (God knows that was all over the ship), but just in terms of keeping them in the loop, with regard to things like the autopsy. They had served with her for over a year; they deserved to know what was going on. Bishop especially—he, more than anyone else in the armory crew, had always treated her fairly. Never pressed her to do things that made her uncomfortable, or tried to dig up the past.

Unlike me, Reed thought, remembering.

I couldn't leave it alone.

Four

BRIDGE
1/03/2151 1744 HOURS

Hᴇ ᴡᴀꜱ ꜱᴛᴀʀɪɴɢ ᴀᴛ ᴀ ᴘɪᴄᴛᴜʀᴇ of Ensign Hart—how
she'd looked back aboard the *Achilles*. A less severe haircut—a less severe expression on her face.

"Lieutenant."

Reed turned hurriedly from the display at his
station to see Sub-Commander T'Pol standing
next to him. He took a quick step forward, block-
ing the display from her view.

"Sub-Commander. What can I do for you?"

"You are making extensive demands on the li-
brary computer system," T'Pol said. "Are these related to your tactical functions?"

"No. They're—ah—personal."

"I see. Could I ask, then, that you limit your
usage for the next hour. In preparation for

our rendezvous with the *Shi'ar*, I would like to consolidate several of our databases in order to maximize the amount of available data storage."

"Sub-Commander, our rendezvous isn't for another few weeks yet," Reed said.

"Two weeks, to be more precise, Lieutenant. Fourteen days, during which I have numerous other tasks to perform, and as most of the crew is otherwise occupied during the dinner hour, I was hoping to get a head start on—"

"All right, all right, I understand," Reed said, reflecting that Vulcans had nothing on the Boy Scouts when it came to being prepared. "I'm going to the mess in a minute as well. Let me just finish up here."

"Thank you. Please let me know when you have completed your task."

He waited until T'Pol had returned to her station before turning back to his screen.

He'd been researching Jon Lyman and the *Achilles*, and what happened at Dinai Station. His memory of the incident had been, for the most part, correct. There had been a raid by pirates at Dinai, a dilithium-refining facility near the Denobulan cluster. The *Achilles* had happened by, and attempted a rescue, with disastrous results. Two hostages (both Vulcans) were killed, the pirates escaped with a fortune in dilithium crystals, and the *Achilles* itself was badly damaged, taking heavy casualties in the process—including her captain.

Yet for all the headlines the incident had generated, there were precious few details about what had actually occurred at the station. Starfleet records were similarly unhelpful—though they did list Ensign Alana Hart as a member of the security team who'd attempted to infiltrate the dilithium facility. But again, there was very little hard information in the files, and what was even more surprising, no eyewitness testimony from the survivors.

Strange. He wondered if there wasn't something concrete hiding behind Hart's reluctance to discuss the past.

Reed closed up the records he'd been studying, and cleared his display.

"All yours, Sub-Commander," he told T'Pol, and left the bridge.

In the mess hall, he caught sight of Trip at a corner table. He got a tray of food and pulled up a chair next to him.

"That's a mistake," Trip said, pointing at Reed's plate.

"Why mistake? The meat loaf is good. I had it yesterday."

"My point exactly. You should've gotten the fried chicken—that's hot out of the skillet."

"Lot of fat in the fried chicken."

"Lot of taste."

"Taste away," Reed said. Trip did just that. Reed pushed his own food around for a moment, then set down his fork.

"Trip—do you ever have problems with anyone on your staff? Fitting in, I mean?"

"Uh-huh."

"Who?"

"All of 'em." He shrugged. "You have good people, you're always going to have some friction when they deal with each other. Especially on a long mission like this, cooped up together day after day after day. The trick is to keep on top of things, keep the lines of communication open, and not to let any bad feelings fester. And make sure you're always the bad guy any time there's a problem." He smiled. "That way they start to hate you, not each other."

"Command one-oh-one, by Charles Tucker the third."

"I'm kidding," Trip said. "About the hate part." He frowned. "We talking about anyone in particular here?"

Reed hesitated. "Hart."

Trip nodded. "Yeah, I've heard things about her. Doesn't play well with others."

"Yes. She's just not fitting in. A bit of a loner—as you suggested."

Trip snorted. "Ain't that the pot calling the kettle black."

"What do you mean by that?"

"I wasn't even sure you had a first name until six months into the mission."

"Very funny." But Reed saw his point.

Trip took another bite of his fried chicken. "She is kinda cute, though."

Reed rolled his eyes. "Not that that's an issue."

"Sometimes it is." Trip set down his chicken, and frowned. "Am I remembering right—she was on *Achilles?*"

"That's correct."

"Well there it is. You gotta give her some time, that's all. That was—" He shook his head, clearly searching for the words. "It must have been hard. I can't imagine."

"It's been a few years since all that, though."

"Something's still bothering her, obviously. You should find out what."

"I've tried. She's managed to miss every meeting we've set up. Either she's covering other people's shifts, working over on her own—"

"She can't be working all the time," Trip said. "You gotta go find her."

Reed nodded. "You're right."

He took a bite of the meat loaf then, and frowned.

Trip was right about that too. It was dry as a bone.

Reed went to the armory after dinner and puttered around for a while. His shift was long over;

the next one was due to start shortly. Hart was scheduled to work it. His initial thought had been to catch her when she came on duty, but he realized now that could backfire. Better to go to her cabin, and talk there.

On his way, he briefly considered getting Hart on the com to warn her he was coming, but quickly decided not to. A surprise visit might make for a little awkwardness, but if he did give her a heads-up, she might end up climbing out the airduct to get away from him.

Not what I envisioned running a department was like, Reed reflected, coming to a stop outside her cabin door.

He buzzed the com.

"Yes?"

"Ensign, it's Lieutenant Reed. May I speak with you a minute?"

There was a long pause—so long that Reed half wondered if she wasn't, in fact, using the airduct to escape him. Then the door slid open. Hart stood in the entrance, a faint flush of color on her face.

"Sir," she said. "I'm sorry—I wasn't expecting you, or I would have answered right away. I was just getting ready to come on duty."

Her hair, he noticed, was down. It was the first time he'd seen her wear it that way. It looked better that way, he thought. Not entirely regulation, but—

"Sir?"

Reed suddenly realized Hart was waiting for him to say something.

"Oh. Ah—may I?" Reed asked, and before she had time to respond, he stepped past her into the cabin. She followed, and the door slid shut behind her.

"I hope you'll forgive the intrusion," Reed said. "But I thought perhaps we could talk for a few minutes."

"Yes, sir. I understand." She stood very still, slumped over, almost, waiting to be rebuked for missing all their previous appointments. Reed didn't think that necessary.

"Is there a place we could sit?" Reed asked, looking around. Like the majority of the crew compartments on this deck, Hart's was a two-person cabin. Her roommate for the first few weeks of the mission had been Cravens from engineering, but Cravens had since decided to bunk elsewhere, leaving Hart all by herself. Which was no doubt how she preferred it.

"Over here," Hart said, leading him to a recessed alcove along the wall. She pulled up a chair for herself, and then one for Reed. They sat down opposite each other.

"So," Reed began. "I wanted to continue our discussion from . . ."

He frowned. There was a shelf set into the bulkhead behind Hart. It held a single picture, and a handful of books. The picture was of an older man and woman—her parents, he guessed. One of the books was an oversized blue volume that looked very familiar. He squinted and made out the words on the spine.

England in the Seven Years' War.

"Corbett?" Reed couldn't believe it. "That's not Corbett, is it, Ensign?"

"Yes, sir. It is." Hart reached up and handed the book down to him. "A facsimile, but still—"

"Good God," Reed said, smiling as he flipped through the pages. "My father gave me a copy of this when I was sixteen years old. I broke the spine on it."

"My aunt gave me mine," Hart said. "When I joined Starfleet. She thought if I was going into the service, I might as well understand how battles were supposed to be fought."

"My father's words exactly. This was the primer for him. He used to quiz me on it, for heaven's sake." Reed shook his head, thinking about those late night skull sessions with his dad. The closest they'd ever been really, studying Corbett, Fuller, Liddell Hart, even a little Churchill.

But mostly Corbett.

"The three c's, remember?" Reed continued. " 'Convoy'—"

"—'contain, and conjunct.' " Hart finished the old maxim for him.

The two looked at each other. Both were smiling now.

"Convoy your ships to protect them from the enemy," Reed said. "Contain the enemy's fleet close to home. And conjunct—conduct joint-forces exercises to speed your operations."

"You have to wonder what Corbett would make of war now," Hart said. "How much technology has changed everything."

"Has it, though? Remember World War Three? What happened to ECON's fleet—gone like that." Reed snapped his fingers.

"Not exactly the same thing, sir," Hart said.

Reed shook his head. "Exactly the same thing."

"I disagree. That was destruction, not containment."

"With the same outcome." Reed shook his head. "Ah, well. My father didn't buy my ideas about that war, either. Or about Starfleet. Pissed him off beyond words when I decided to enlist here rather than in the Royal Navy." Reed continued to flip through the book as he talked. "I haven't thought about this stuff in years—some interesting things here though. . . ."

"Borrow it, if you like."

"No, that's all right. It's in the computer—I can look at it there." He held the book out for her to take back. "Thanks anyway."

"Please, sir—go ahead. It's not the same thing, looking at it on a monitor."

Reed nodded. "You're right, of course." He held up the book. "All right—I will take it. And thank you."

"You're welcome."

Reed settled the book on his lap.

"So," he said, looking up at Hart.

And just like that, the comfortable rapport between the two of them was gone, and Reed was acutely aware of what he'd come here to talk about.

So, from the look in her eyes, was Ensign Hart.

"You've gone to a lot of trouble the last few days to avoid talking to me, Ensign," he said. "I've been trying to figure out why."

Hart's head was bowed, and her hands were in her lap. She twisted her fingers together nervously.

"I'm sorry, sir. I—I try not to think about the *Achilles* too much, sir. Or Captain Lyman."

"I can understand that," Reed said. "Some painful memories there, I'm sure."

"Yes, sir."

"But some good ones as well?"

"Yes, but . . . they're not as—present in my mind. I just remember the others."

"What happened at Dinai."

She nodded. "Yes, sir."

"I've been reviewing those records—as many of them as I could lay my hands on," Reed said. "And there's not a lot of detail there. I can't figure out exactly what happened."

"*Achilles* happened to be in the area. We made a routine call in to the station, and the commander responded with a coded SOS. We tried to help, but . . ."

She sighed heavily, and stood. She walked to the small window at the far end of her quarters. Reed followed her there.

"How did you try to help? That's what the records don't say."

"It was a rescue mission," Hart answered, her back to him. "It went wrong."

"How?"

She shook her head. "I can't say."

"You mean you can't remember?"

"No, I—" She shook her head. "I'm sorry, sir."

Reed studied her profile. She *was* sorry, he saw. More than sorry, in fact. The expression on her face was one of anguish.

"Ensign, what happened out there? Tell me."

She shook her head again. Her eyes glistened with tears. "I can't. I'm not supposed to."

Reed was stunned into silence for a moment.

"Not supposed to?" he asked finally. "Who says you're not supposed to? Starfleet?" Which would explain the lack of detail in the records— possibly the newsfeeds as well, but still. . . . "Why?"

"Oh, please, sir," she said, turning to him suddenly. "Please don't ask me about this any more. Please."

"Ensign, something is obviously bothering you a great deal, and—"

"I can't talk about it, sir," she repeated. "Please."

Reed looked at her and realized Hart wasn't going to say anything more about Dinai, no matter how hard he pressed.

"All right." Reed said. "We won't discuss it right now."

Which didn't mean he was giving up. He was going to get the answers he wanted, and soon. Not just for the sake of satisfying his curiosity, either. For Ensign Hart, because whatever had happened, keeping it a secret was tearing her up inside. It was a wound as raw as any he'd ever come across, and it was five years old and festering. It had to be exposed to fresh air and allowed to heal. But not tonight.

Tonight he'd settle for taking a much smaller step toward helping integrate Hart into the crew.

"Hart—what happened on the *Achilles*—I can accept that you can't, or won't, tell me about it. That's fine. What I can't accept is that incident affecting your performance aboard *Enterprise*. And you shouldn't accept it affecting the rest of your life."

Hart nodded. "Yes, sir. You're right, sir."

"Please," Reed said. "You can stop calling me sir all the time. Lieutenant will do as well."

"All right," Hart said. "Lieutenant it is."

The two of them stood, still facing each other.

"Hart—when I was reviewing the information on Dinai—I also took the time to pull your service record. And I found that you're an expert marksman—top five in your class at the Academy. Yet you haven't even attempted to qualify on the new phase pistols."

"No, sir." Hart was avoiding his gaze again. "I didn't think it necessary—since I hadn't asked to be on any of the away missions."

"There may be other situations that arise where you need to use that weapon. You should prepare for them."

"I suppose you're right," she said.

"Of course I am. We'll meet in the armory—tomorrow morning, before breakfast. I'll show you the weapon then, and we can conduct a little drill—all right?"

"All right."

Reed smiled. "Good."

Hart smiled back—not as big a smile as she'd given him before, when they were talking about Corbett, but a smile nonetheless.

"And thank you for the book, again."

"You're welcome. I enjoyed our discussion—about Corbett, anyway." Her smile fell away a little, and Reed knew she was thinking about Dinai again.

"Ensign," he said sharply. "The past will fade—eventually. I'm sure of it."

53

"Yes, sir."

"Ah." Reed held up a warning finger. "Lieutenant—remember?"

"Right. Lieutenant." She hesitated. "Thank you for talking to me. I do appreciate it."

"Not at all. I feel as if I've fallen down on the job a little, to tell you the truth, taking so long to do it."

"No, no. The fault's been mine."

"Well. Regardless . . ." Reed nodded. "I should get going. You're on duty in a moment."

"Not for a few moments actually."

She sounded, suddenly, anxious to prolong the conversation. Reed wondered why. Then he looked closely at her, and got it.

Hart was lonely.

But looking at her, he was also suddenly very aware of something else. Starfleet regulations, in particular one from the officers' code of conduct.

No fraternization between officers and the crew.

Reed cleared his throat. "No, ah—not to rush off, but I do have some things to attend to. Good night, Ensign."

"Yes, of course. Good night, Lieutenant."

Reed stopped at the door, and turned back to her.

"Tomorrow morning in the armory. You're going to be there, aren't you?"

"Yes, sir," she said, and smiled again. "I promise."

"Good. I'll see you then."

Reed fell asleep that night reading in bed, the Corbett propped open on his lap.

But more than the book, Reed remembered his thoughts had been of the woman who'd given it to him.

Five

CABIN C-423
1/16/2151 1924 HOURS

REED PUSHED THE MEMORIES FROM HIS MIND and entered the cell. The prisoner and Valay were going at it full tilt, yelling at each other through the mesh screen that split the room in two.

"Ma'ar tachee galla."

"Ma tee taba lee."

"Ma'ar k'tanga kol nitachee haruka!"

Reed made his way to the captain's side.

"What language are they speaking?" he asked.

"The prisoner's," Archer said. "Hoshi's on it."

Reed saw. She stood next to the captain, her hands flying across the translator padd.

The cell was an unfinished compartment in the crew's quarters, stripped of everything except a bunk and a workstation for the prisoner to eat meals at, separated from the rest of the cell by the floor-to-ceiling sheet of wire mesh. In case the prisoner managed somehow to tear away the mesh, they'd sealed the room's ventilation shaft and disabled computer access. He would have been trapped anyway. And if he had somehow managed to get the door open, there were the guards to get past.

All of which had been moot points considering that up until early this morning, the prisoner had been unconscious. In a coma. No longer. Now he was shouting at the ambassador as if his life depended on it.

Which just might be the case, Reed realized.

"Hoshi?" Archer asked. "How much longer?"

"A few more seconds," she replied without looking up from the padd. "The two languages—Sarkassian and Ta'alaat—are not related at all. The Ta'alaat phonemes do seem to have a lot in common with—" She frowned at which she was seeing on the padd, and shook her head. "Hajjlaran ones? That's odd. What we know about Hajjlaran civilization—"

"Hoshi," Archer interrupted. "Let's save the etymology for later, and concentrate on the task at hand."

"Yes, sir," Hoshi said. "Should have it right about—now."

And suddenly, the translator began to render Valay's words into English.

". . . for every life you took. In fact, unless those

57

who aided you come forward, I promise that what happened at Dar Shalaan will seem like a mild punishment."

A thin smile crossed the prisoner's face. "Violence only begets violence, Ambassador. As I hoped you and yours would have learned by now."

The prisoner was humanoid as well. Shorter, stockier than the Sarkassians, he had slightly darker skin, with a bluish tinge to it. That bluish tinge had not been there when they'd brought the man aboard—Reed was sure of it. Which made him wonder if there wasn't something to Dr. Natir's earlier statement that the prisoner had used drugs to alter his appearance.

"You are going to pay for what you've done," the ambassador responded. "I promise you that."

The captain moved forward.

"Excuse me, Ambassador," he said. "My turn to talk to this man, I think."

"Talk is a waste of time," she said, stepping back. "But—as you wish."

The captain took her place at the screen.

"My name is Jonathan Archer," he said. "I'm captain of this vessel."

"I am Goridian," the prisoner said.

"He admits that much, at least," Valay muttered.

"I don't know you," the captain continued. "But these people here, the Sarkassians, have accused you of destroying their outpost—murdering their scientists. They want me to turn you over to them."

"Instead of questioning me," Goridian said, raising his voice, "why don't you ask these Sarkassians"—he used the word like a curse, practically spitting it out—"what deaths they have to their credit? Why don't you ask them what their scientists were doing there? Why don't you—"

"We do not target innocent civilians!" Valay shot back, standing right at the captain's shoulder. "We do not wage war on an entire population!"

"Now who lies?" Goridian said. "How could anyone look at what you have done to my people, and not call it war?"

"Give myself and Doctor Natir five minutes with this man, Captain," Ambassador Valay said. "We will get you your answers."

"That's not how we do things around here," Archer said. "Mister Goridian, I answered a distress signal in a good faith effort to save lives. Instead, one of my crew is dead, and I can't help but suspect that what happened down at the outpost had something to do with it."

"I am sorry for your loss, Captain. But I did not kill your crewman," Goridian said. And then he did something very strange.

He looked past Archer, and right at Reed.

"I am sure you will discover who did," Goridian said.

And as their eyes met for the first time, Reed felt his whole body tense up in anger.

Goridian was lying. The man knew exactly what had happened to Alana.

But how was that possible? Goridian had been unconscious—in a coma—when Hart had died. There was no way he could know what had taken place.

The prisoner's gaze left him, and found Roan, standing next to Reed.

"Captain Roan. I had heard they put you out to pasture."

"Commodore now, I'm afraid, Goridian."

"All these titles. I prefer the one my people know you by best. Butcher."

"Strange words coming from one with your record."

"I have a long way to go to catch up with you."

"If you hope to make me lose my temper, I'm afraid you're doomed to fail. If you want to make me feel guilty about Dar Shalaan, there is no need."

"Your pretensions to a conscience are too little, too late, Commodore. History has already sat in judgment on your deeds."

"And what will history have to say about yours, Goridian?"

"All right, Commodore," Archer said. "Let's stop trading accusations, please."

He turned to Goridian then.

"Now. Let's have your story."

They questioned the prisoner at length, Valay first, and then the captain. In the middle of the interrogation, Goridian asked for something to drink. Phlox handed him a thermos full of a greenish, foamy liquid.

"This contains all the necessary nutrients for your species in easily digestible form. I suspect it will quench your thirst as well."

Goridian had just finished admitting—no, *admitting* was the wrong term, boasting was what he'd done—of intentionally destroying the Sarkassian outpost.

"And then I waited," he said to Valay. "Waited for your ships to come, to rescue your scientists. I waited, and I hid. I expected to be found. I expected to die—and I wanted to take as many of you with me as I could."

He took another sip of the liquid, and swirled it around his mouth. Reed watched him, and marveled. The man talked about murder the same way Reed talked about taking a shower. Reed found it chilling.

He wondered what the two races—Sarkassians and Ta'alaat—had done to each other over the years to inspire such hatred. He wondered what Roan had done at Dar Shalaan, and why Goridian had called him "Butcher."

And most of all, he wondered what had really happened down at the outpost.

Because Goridian's powers of observation had failed him when it came to describing what had happened to Ensign Hart.

"There was an explosion," he had said. "And I woke up aboard your ship."

Archer had pressed him. But Goridian had offered nothing else.

"I must say," the captain pointed out, "I find parts of your story less than believable."

"You see, Captain," Valay said. "You will never get truth from this man."

The captain was silent a long time before speaking.

"I'm beginning to agree with you, Ambassador. Mister Goridian, perhaps I should turn you over to the Sarkassians," Archer said. "Their methods of interrogation might jog your memory a little bit more effectively than mine seem to."

"I can assure you of that," Ambassador Valay said.

"Then . . ." Archer shrugged. "I believe that's what I'll do."

"Sir, I must protest," Phlox said. "You are aware that they mean to use torture on this man?"

"Doctor, please," Archer said. "I think I know what I'm doing."

Reed thought he knew as well. The captain was forcing Goridian's hand. Of course, if Goridian knew what kind of man the captain was, he would know Archer's was an empty threat. But the alien didn't know that. He couldn't know that. Only Archer's crew could know him that way.

Reed looked over at the prisoner, expecting to see emotions such as fear or surprise, perhaps even anger on Goridian's face.

But Goridian stood in front of his bunk, looking unfazed by the captain's threat.

Reed was confused. Either Goridian was a very cool customer, or . . .

"Well, Mister Goridian?" the captain asked. "Are you prepared to tell us the truth about what happened? Or would you prefer to talk to the ambassador? And Doctor Natir?"

Archer and the prisoner locked eyes.

In that moment, Reed sensed that Goridian was not going to reveal anything more than he already had. It made no sense.

"I have told you what I know, Captain." He shrugged. "I can do no more."

Ambassador Valay was smiling.

"You are making the correct decision, Captain. And I can assure you, whatever information we do obtain from this man we will share with you."

"I appreciate that." Archer stared at Goridian. Reed knew the captain was going to have to go back on his word, and tell the ambassador that Goridian would have to remain aboard *Enterprise*.

But the prisoner spoke first.

"Ambassador Valay, perhaps we should talk."

"I am sure we will." Valay smiled. "At some length, in fact."

"I mean now," Goridian said. "Alone."

Reed and Archer exchanged surprised expressions.

Valay laughed. "What could you possibly have to say to me that you could not say in front of all these people?"

"A message from our leadership to you."

Valay, for the first time since Reed had met her, fell silent for a moment.

"And you wait till now to tell me?"

Goridian nodded. "You'll see why—once you dismiss these others."

Reed looked from one of them to the other. He saw nothing but anger in Valay's eyes. In Goridian's eyes, though . . .

Where he would have expected to see fear, he saw the cold light of calculation.

Don't trust him, a little voice in his head said.

"If you are wasting my time . . ." Valay said.

"I promise you," the prisoner said. "You will want to hear this."

"Just a minute," Captain Archer said. "I don't like this idea."

"I fail to see how it concerns you," Goridian said.

"For once, I agree." Valay turned toward the captain, hands clasped behind her back.

At that moment, Hoshi stepped forward and spoke quietly into the captain's ear. He nodded as she talked.

"All right," Archer said when she'd finished. "I still don't like it. But if the ambassador agrees . . ."

"It will probably be a wasted five minutes, but . . ." She shrugged. "I will listen."

"Good." Goridian looked from the captain to Hoshi. "I hope you are not planning to listen as well, Captain. With some kind of listening device."

"No," Archer said. "We don't do that sort of thing."

"Very well. If you will excuse us then . . ."

Archer turned without another word and left the cabin. Hoshi and Phlox followed him out. Roan and Natir went next.

Which left Reed alone with Valay and Goridian.

"Lieutenant?" the ambassador said. "Do you have something you wish to add?"

"Yes," Reed said, looking at Goridian. The man's actions, his whole manner—the cat who ate the canary—troubled him. "Be careful, Ambassador."

With that, Reed left the cabin.

Outside, Captain Archer stood several feet away from the cell entrance, talking with Hoshi, who had her head bowed.

"Sir," Reed said, crossing to the two of them. "I have to think that Goridian—"

Archer held up a hand. "Wait." He turned back to Hoshi. "Anything yet?"

"No, sir," she replied. Reed saw now she had her padd out in front of her and was studying it intently.

For a second, Reed thought the captain had gone back on his word and was actually spying on what was happening inside the cell.

Archer must have seen the look on his face.

"What Valay and Goridian were saying before the translator started working—it's in there," the captain said quietly. "Hoshi's trying to find and translate it. That may give us a little more information. Some kind of clue as to what Goridian's up to."

Hoshi grunted in frustration.

"What's the matter?"

"I downloaded the entire Hajjlaran language database into this unit right after they started talking. The index is all—messed up. It'll take a few minutes to find that conversation."

"Fast as you can," Archer said. "I want to know what they said."

"Aye, sir."

"Captain," Reed said. "Do you want me to go back in there?"

"No. That's not necessary. I just . . ." He shook his head, and stared at the closed cabin door. "I just don't like not knowing what's going on."

"Neither do I," Reed said. His hand went unconsciously to his side, where he would normally wear a phase pistol, and he had the sudden, irrational thought that he should go to the armory, fast as he could, get one out of the weapons locker, and hurry back here, to the cell.

Which was silly. No reason for him to need a phase pistol here and now.

And yet . . .

His fingers twitched, searching for the grip. Thoughts of the weapon wouldn't leave his head.

Six

THE PHASE PISTOL LAY on the main firing console
before him, fully charged, its barrel shining, looking sleek, ready—almost eager—for use.

Reed felt like apologizing to it.

Sorry, my friend. No action for you today.

He brought the armory lights back up and used
the remote control to switch off the holographic
targeting device.

Hart was almost twenty minutes late now.
Late—why gild the lily?

It was clear she wasn't coming at all.

He couldn't believe it. He really thought he was
getting through to her last night—leaving aside
their unfinished discussion about the *Achilles* and
Dinai Station, he thought the two of them had
reached an understanding, had agreed that she

needed to take steps toward becoming more involved with life aboard *Enterprise*.

Part of him also thought they'd made a more personal connection as well—the start of a real friendship, having found some common ground in the Corbett volume and their separate histories.

It hurt to think he'd been wrong.

Reed turned toward the com then, intending to locate her and have her report to his quarters, get the situation straightened out.

Which was exactly when the armory door slid open, and Hart strode quickly inside.

"I'm so sorry, sir," she said. "I overslept. It's never happened to me before, and I promise it won't again."

Reed looked at her and frowned. *Overslept?* he wanted to say. Hart looked to him, in fact, as if she hadn't slept at all. There were dark circles under her eyes, and her hair, rather than being pulled into a tight regulation bun, was tied back in a simple ponytail. Her coverall was rumpled as well—she looked as if she'd just gotten out of bed.

"Perhaps there's another time we can do this," Reed said. "You were on late last night, so—"

"Oh, no, it's not that, sir. I just had trouble falling asleep."

Reed thought he understood.

"Nervous about doing this?"

"Well—a little, I suppose."

"That's only natural. We still have a little time—as long as you don't mind rushing through breakfast."

"Not at all," Hart said.

"All right. Then let's get started."

Hart was somewhat familiar with the phase pistol already—she knew how to load it and check the charge, both of which were part of her armory duties. It was easy enough to show her how to change between the weapon's two settings (stun and kill), and how to modify it so that it acted as more of a targeting laser. Which they needed to do for the drills Reed had in mind.

"So," he said, taking the pistol from her and holding it in his hand. "To fire this—the most important thing to remember is that it's not like any of the particle weapons you're used to. No need to compensate for drift. No falloff of the beam's intensity over any distance you're likely to fire. It's as true as a laser—even more so, in fact. You just point," he aimed the phaser at an imaginary target on the far wall, "and fire."

"Sounds pretty straightforward," Hart said.

"It is. Ready for a little target practice?"

"I think so."

"Good." He handed the pistol back to her, and picked up the remote control for the targeting device again. He lowered the room lights, and powered on the target.

Twenty feet above them, toward the rear of the armory, an octagonal yellow target about the size of a softball suddenly appeared—or rather, seemed to appear. It was actually a holographic image, projected into the room by the device fastened to the wall behind it.

Hart picked up the phaser, and sighted along it.

"Let's try a ten-second firing window first," Reed said, punching up the settings for that drill.

The device began jetting about the room.

Hart sighted along the pistol, and fired. Once, twice, a third time.

All misses.

She fired again, and again, and again.

"Time," Reed called.

The device came to a sudden stop, hovering expectantly.

Reed looked down at the display on the remote. "One hit, twenty-one misses."

Hart shook her head in disgust. "God, I'm out of practice," she said, almost as if she couldn't believe it herself.

Reed nodded. Her motions were stiff and unnatural. She was thinking, trying to anticipate the target's movements in her mind, rather than reacting to them instinctively.

"Can't expect miracles, Ensign. Not right away at least. Let's try again."

They did. Her reflexes started to come back.

She began to move more like the expert marksman her records showed she'd been—her motions fluid and compact, no wasted motion, the pistol moving from side to side, her shoulders relaxed, her right foot slightly forward, knees barely bent, left arm relaxed at her side. Textbook firing position. A smile crossed his face. She was a pleasure to watch.

Hart stepped back, and wiped her brow. "How was that, sir?"

Reed suddenly realized he'd been paying a lot more attention to her than the scores coming through on the remote.

"Better," he said quickly. "About fifty-fifty hit-to-miss ratio."

"I can do better."

Reed nodded and reset the device. But a dozen trials in, Hart seemed to be stuck at the same percentage. He could see she was starting to get frustrated, too—he didn't want that. This exercise was supposed to build her confidence back up, not tear it down.

He walked behind her, and sighted along the target as she did. He saw what the problem was immediately. She was still compensating for particle drift—shooting as if the pistol wouldn't fire entirely true. It was probably completely unconscious on her part—more like a muscle memory than anything else.

He powered down the targeting projector.

"Sir?"

"Here," he said, walking back toward her. "Let me show you something."

Hoshi had this same problem with the drift—worse, in fact, and in the end, to help her qualify on the pistol, he'd had to physically correct the ever-so-slight tendency she had to compensate: take her hand in his, and stop the errant motion as she started to fire. That's what he'd decided to do with Hart.

Except that as he came up alongside her, all of a sudden he was nervous. About touching her.

Don't be ridiculous, he told himself. *This isn't a date.*

"Let's forget about this exercise a moment—see the monitor, at the top of the stairs there?"

He nodded toward the auxiliary workstation on the upper level at the rear of the armory.

"Yes."

"The corner of the display—upper-right corner, let's say—that's our target."

"I don't understand."

"You're still compensating for particle drift," he explained. "I want to try and make you aware of it. I'll target the phase pistol, then you fire."

"How does that work?" Hart asked.

"Like this," Reed said. "Here."

He took Hart's right hand in his, and raised it along with the pistol.

He was very aware of her face, scant inches

away, and his hand, wrapped tightly around hers.

He shifted position to get the monitor in his sight, and their hips brushed.

"Sorry," he said.

"It's all right."

Concentrate, Reed told himself, and sighted up the barrel.

"Fire," he said.

Hart squeezed the trigger, and the beam hit the monitor square in the center.

"My fault," he said. "One more time."

He focused on the target again.

"Fi—"

"One second," Hart said, and raised her left hand to brush away a lock of hair that had fallen in front of her face. "Damn. Sorry. Hold on a minute."

She stepped back, and pulled her hair entirely out of the ponytail. It cascaded down her shoulders.

"Rat's nest," she said, pulling it back again. "Ought to get it all cut off."

"Don't," Reed said, the word escaping his lips before he was even consciously aware of thinking it. He looked at Hart and flushed. "I mean—"

She smiled. "It's all right. I know what you mean."

Their eyes met, and he saw that she did.

"Should we try it again?" she asked.

"Yes," Reed said. "Only without the phase pistol."

He took a step forward. So did she.

And then they were kissing.

After some time, they pulled apart.

Now it was Reed's turn to brush a lock of hair away from her face.

"How was that?" Hart asked.

He smiled. "Right on target."

"Should we try again, sir?"

"Not so many 'sirs,' remember?"

"All right." She looked up at him. "You have to cut down on the 'ensigns' then."

"Fair enough."

"My name's Alana," she added quickly. "At the Academy, though, everybody called me Laney. Or just Hart."

"Everyone always called me 'Reed'—even my parents, I think."

They both laughed.

"What is your first name? If it's not out of line for me to ask."

"Malcolm, actually," he heard himself say, and then at the same time, he heard another little voice in his head.

Way out of line, it whispered. *Regulations.*

The com sounded.

"Archer to Lieutenant Reed. Archer to Reed."

Reed started like he'd just grabbed hold of a joy buzzer.

"Excuse me," he said to Hart, and hurried across the room to the nearest com.

"Reed here."

"We need you up here, Malcolm."

"On my way. Out."

He closed the channel. Hart stood a few feet away from him, still holding the phase pistol.

"I have to go—can you—"

"I'll clean things up, yes." She paused a moment. "I have the same shift this evening."

"I'm up late," Reed said quickly. "I'll call you."

Her face fell, ever so slightly. "All right," she said.

He hurried out of the armory, and onto the turbolift, thinking about the kiss and the little voice in his head and wondering what in the world he was going to do next.

For the first time in his life, Starfleet regulations made absolutely no sense to him.

One deck up, the turbolift stopped. Trip got on.

"Who died?" he asked.

"What?"

"You look like you're comin' from your best friend's funeral. What's wrong?"

"Oh—nothing. Just thinking."

"Yeah, I can tell that. About what?"

Reed hesitated. Trip was just about his closest friend on the ship. He'd always been able to talk to him about anything.

"Ensign Hart," he said—and right then, the turbolift door opened onto the bridge.

Trip nodded thoughtfully. "We'll talk later, all right?"

"All right," Reed said, and they stepped forward onto the bridge.

Enterprise had come across a marker buoy of some sort. It self-destructed before they could get a detailed scan of it. T'Pol thought it might have sent off a signal; Reed analyzed the explosion to see if he could come to any sort of conclusions about the level of technology they were dealing with.

Two hours on, they were able to finally pull together some low-resolution images of what the buoy had looked like intact, by extrapolating from the readings they had managed to get.

It resembled nothing so much as a small pyramid. Strange symbols—hieroglyphs of some sort—covered its surface.

"Now, that's interesting," Hoshi said.

She was still on the bridge, hard at work trying to decipher those symbols, when Reed left, just before midnight. He'd spent fifteen hours straight at his station, breaking only to use the head and stretch his legs. Someone had passed around sandwiches—he vaguely remember eating a couple.

Ensign Hart—Alana—had barely crossed his mind the whole time.

Back in his quarters, though . . .

She was all he could think about.

He thought about calling her. He thought about calling Trip.

He picked up the Corbett, and tried to read.

Finally, he just went to sleep. It took a long while. He dreamt. He was in the ready room, talking to Captain Archer.

"You wanted to see me, Malcolm?"

"Yes, sir. Well, sir, it's about Ensign Hart. She and I—"

"How's she working out? I noticed she hasn't been on any of the landing parties yet."

"No, sir. But we've been drilling with the phase pistols, sir, and I think she's getting it. Fairly soon, she should be ready."

"Good. How's her state of mind? The Achilles, and all that?"

"Better. I think she's working through what happened, and I'm—"

"Well, have Phlox do a psychological workup on her. Don't you get involved in playing counselor, Malcolm. Too much temptation to abuse your position as her superior officer. That's why we have those regulations, you know."

"Regulations."

"Against officers fraternizing with their subordinates. Very important rule."

"Yes, sir."

"Good. Now—was there something else? About you and Ensign Hart?"

"No, sir. Not at all."

At some point, Reed remembered waking up and going to his workstation. He'd found a message from Ensign Hart. Alana.

Practice again in the armory? 0800?

He'd thought long and hard, formulating a response in his mind, seeing her face before him. Then Reed sat down, and began to type.

Seven

CORRIDOR, C-DECK
1/16/2151 1924 HOURS

THE SOFT CLICK OF THE KEYS faded, replaced by the ever-present hiss of the air-circulation system.

"They don't look any more comfortable with this than I am."

Reed turned and saw Captain Archer looking past him down the corridor, to where Commodore Roan and Dr. Natir stood, heads bowed together, talking in hushed tones.

"See if you can find out why they're concerned," Archer suggested.

"Yes, sir."

Reed walked over to the two Sarkassians.

"Gentlemen."

Both inclined their heads in greeting. Reed turned to Natir. "I wonder if I could have a moment alone with the commodore."

Natir looked annoyed. "I suppose so."

"Perhaps Doctor Phlox could give you a tour of our sickbay," Reed suggested.

"I need no tour," Natir said. "Excuse me."

The doctor huffed off.

Roan shook his head, a slight grin on his face. "You'll forgive the lack of diplomacy, I hope, Lieutenant. It is not Doctor Natir's field of expertise."

"I would agree with that," Reed said. *And what's the ambassador's excuse?* he thought.

"We are all under a considerable amount of stress at the moment," Roan added, as if he'd read the lieutenant's thoughts. "Will you please convey that to the captain."

"Of course. I'm sure he understands already."

"Thank you." Roan hesitated a second. "If you're here to ask me what Goridian might have to say to our ambassador, I can assure you I am as much in the dark as you are."

"That partially. Though—it seems you and the prisoner know each other?"

"Ah. I see the 'Butcher' reference did not escape you."

"No."

Roan nodded. "We know of each other would be a more accurate way to put it."

"Dar Shalaan."

"Dar Shalaan, yes."

Reed waited a moment, hoping Roan would

continue. But the commodore seemed, suddenly, lost in a world of his own.

"I can't say I've had a lot of experience doing this, Commodore. Establishing relations between two cultures. One thing I have learned, though, is that as some point, trust must always enter into the equation."

"Of course," Roan said. "Such has been my experience as well."

Reed moved closer, and lowered his voice. "The captain and I—Starfleet on the whole, in fact—have an interest in helping you and the Ta'alaat find a way toward peace. But to do that, you need to tell us what you are fighting about."

Roan sighed. "Everything. We are fighting about everything, Lieutenant."

"That doesn't tell me much."

"Territory. Resources. History." Roan's eyes grew hard. "Or perhaps I should just say religion, and have done with it."

"Religion?"

Roan nodded. "To hear them tell it, we have desecrated their holy places, stolen treasures given to them by their gods. We live in areas promised to them by divine providence."

Reed was silent a moment. What Roan was telling him—this was not good. Conflicts over territory and resources could be resolved by compromise—a piece of this to one side, a piece of that to the other. History could be overcome by establishing new patterns of behavior. But religion . . .

Earth's own history was full of bloody wars of cultural genocide, complete annihilation by one side of the other. Those who did not share the same beliefs were deemed less than human, and slaughtered. Most of those wars, however, had been fought with swords and spears, guns and grenades—rarely with weapons of the sophistication and destructive capability both the Sarkassians and the Ta'alaat apparently possessed.

Reed was beginning to get an idea of how dangerous this fight was.

"We have been fighting the Ta'alaat for centuries," Roan said. "Thousands have died."

"At places like Dar Shalaan."

Roan nodded. "Yes. The war has gone on so long—there are those on both sides who no longer think peace is possible. Valay is one of them."

"And she's your ambassador?"

"Well." Roan leaned closer. "May I speak confidentially, Lieutenant?"

Reed shook his head. "I have to be able to share what I learn with the captain."

Roan nodded. "Yes. That would be all right."

He drew Reed farther down the corridor, away from the others.

"Valay serves as ambassador more as a result of circumstance than anything else—not by training. Or temperament. Quite the opposite, in fact. She is the closest thing we have to royalty on our world. Here and now—she represents one point of view among my people. A very popular point of view now, I must say, though not one I entirely agree with."

"One with a pessimistic view of the war between your peoples."

"Exactly." Roan smiled wryly. "Unfortunately, I think you can tell whose point of view currently holds sway."

As if on cue, the cell door hissed open. Ambassador Valay strode out. The ornamental band—the crown—that had held her hair back was gone, and a second later Reed saw that she was carrying it in her hand. He also noticed a spattering of dark stains on the front of her robe. Odd. He hadn't seen them before.

Valay swept the hall with her gaze, and stopped when she found Roan.

"Goridian is dead," the ambassador said. "We are leaving."

For a split second, the corridor fell silent.

Then it erupted into pandemonium.

Reed was the first one into the cell. He didn't know what he expected to find.

The mesh grid was intact. Goridian lay slumped on the floor next to it, one hand still gripping the wire. His eyes were wide with surprise. His blood coated the floor. It was red. For some reason, that stuck with Reed. Most of the aliens they'd met bled in different colors.

"Open this!" Phlox stood next to Reed, grabbing at the screen.

Bishop rushed in. Seconds later, Phlox was through the gate, kneeling next to the prisoner, tricorder in hand.

"No respiratory activity, no autonomic function. Massive"—and here the doctor's voice registered momentary confusion—"neurological disruption. Cause of death," Phlox said, "trauma here, and here."

He pointed to the prisoner's eyes. But he didn't need to. Everyone—Reed included—could see how Goridian had died.

Reed spun around, and saw the crown Valay held in her hands.

The ends came to sharp, sticky, shiny points.

Reed turned to the captain, who stood in the doorway, looking from Goridian's body to Valay.

Archer seemed at a loss for words.

Roan wasn't. "Valay. You—what have you done?"

"His so-called offer to me was an insult. His presence here, alive, an even greater one." She shrugged. "We are at war. And I have killed one of the enemy. That is what I have done."

"You—" Roan was so angry, he actually sputtered. "You have done far more than that. You have abused the hospitality of—" He shook his head, clearly trying to control himself. "Captain Archer, on behalf of the Sarkassian government, I apologize most deeply for the ambassador's actions and—"

"Have a care, Commodore," Valay said. "I speak for the Sarkassian government. And you remember who you are speaking to. Who you take your orders from."

"I take my orders from the Central Council of our government, Ambassador. Who will be as angry with you as I am when they hear of this."

"I think not, Commodore. Remember, I take my orders from them as well." She turned to Dr. Natir. "Come. We are returning to the outpost."

"No." Captain Archer stepped forward, having found his voice. He looked as angry as Reed had ever seen him. "Not just yet you're not. You cannot just walk aboard my ship and kill someone."

Valay regarded the captain impassively. "As I told you from the beginning, this affair was between us and the Sarkassians. Ta'alaat, excuse me. Between Goridian and myself. And now it is over."

"And I say it isn't. Not yet," Archer said. "If I can't get my answers from Goridian, I'll have to get them from you."

"I'm afraid not, Captain."

"I'm afraid so. You will tell me the purpose of your outpost, Ambassador." Archer stepped forward, till he stood inches away from the ambassador. They glared at each other. "I insist on it."

Bishop's hand went slowly to his phase pistol.

Valay noticed. "Perhaps you wish to be a part of our war, Captain? I know many of our ship captains would be happy to accommodate you."

Archer stood for a moment.

"Go," he said finally. "Now. Mister Reed, Mister Bishop—you'll escort the Sarkassians directly to their ship."

"Aye, sir." Reed nodded to Roan. "This way, all of you."

He led them down the corridor toward the turbolift, and then to the shuttlebay. The direct route, this time, the fastest way possible. Roan walked next to him in silence the whole way.

When they reached the shuttlebay, Valay, then Natir stepped through the airlock into their ship without a word. Roan hung back a second.

"This action would never have been ordered by the government," he said quietly. "Valay acted alone."

"I hope you're right," Reed said.

Roan's eyes met his. "I am certain of it. Trust me, Lieutenant."

Then he was through the portal, and out of sight. Reed's eyes lingered a moment on the spot where Roan had stood.

"*It is over,*" Valay had said. But in Reed's experience, that moment—when you thought things were finished, ended, irrevocably complete—was exactly when they started up again, in ways you couldn't have imagined.

He shuddered involuntarily, and his mind, unbidden, summoned up the past again.

Eight

THIS MORNING, THEY WERE BOTH EARLY.

"Ensign," he said quietly, entering the armory and finding her waiting there.

She looked up and smiled at him—a rather forced smile, he thought.

"Lieutenant Reed. Hello."

He saw that she'd already gotten out the phase pistol, and attached the targeting projector on the back wall. The remote lay on the console before him.

"Before we get started," he began. "About yesterday—"

"It's all right sir. No need to say anything. I read your message. It was just the moment, that's all. I understand."

"It wasn't just the moment, Ensign. Alana." He

sighed. "That's what I was trying to say. I think you and I—under different circumstances, we could be—we could have—"

"Sir, you don't need to explain any further. Really. Regulations, I do understand." She smiled that same forced smile again, and Reed felt suddenly sick to his stomach, realizing that at least part of his imaginary dialogue with Archer had some basis in fact. He *had* abused his position, and he'd hurt her, and he couldn't think of a single thing to say that could change that.

"Shall we get started?" she asked.

"Yes, all right." He forced a smile now. "Back to business."

"We should use the projector, don't you think?"

"No," he said, shaking his head, and before she could infer that he wanted to return to the drill that had ended in their kiss yesterday, he quickly continued. "I was thinking of something else entirely."

He went and got one of the old EM-33s from the weapons locker.

"Let's go back to a weapon that has the particle drift," he continued, holding out the gun to her. "Maybe that way you can see the difference in the two weapons for yourself."

"That's an EM-33."

"Yes. I saw in your records that you'd—"

He stopped talking, because even in the dim light he could tell that Hart had gone quite pale.

"Alana? Are you all right?"

"Yes." She nodded mechanically. "I know the 33. That's what we used on *Achilles.*"

Reed, realizing his mistake, cursed himself for an idiot.

He set the gun down.

"That was stupid. I'm sorry. It was thoughtless of me not to realize what the EM-33 might signify to you."

"It's all right, sir."

"No, it's not." He heard an edge in his voice he hadn't meant to put there, and shook his head. "Listen. Alana—you should find someone you can talk about all this with."

"I can't. I explained—"

"Doctor Phlox," Reed interrupted. "Whatever sort of reasons you have for not speaking to me, or your shipmates, they can't apply to him. He's an advisor—plus I believe confidentiality would apply. Doctor-patient privilege."

"I suppose so," she said. "Though—when I was on administrative duty back at Fleet headquarters, they had me talking to a couple of the doctors there. And they didn't really help, to be honest with you."

"Fleet doctors," Reed said. "I think Doctor Phlox would be different."

"It's not that they were Starfleet. It's that—I don't see how a doctor could understand the sorts of things we have to go through. The psychology of being out there, in a life-or-death situation."

"I see your point," Reed said. "But Phlox isn't like that. I promise you."

"All right." Alana didn't sound convinced—but Reed decided not to force the issue. Instead, they continued with the drills using the holographic projector—that day, and the next. Hart's scores rose. They didn't talk about *Achilles*, or Corbett, or themselves, or anything but the phase pistols.

At dinner that evening, Reed managed to brush Trip's questions about Alana off by saying the problem had been resolved. He even agreed to help with some work in engineering the next day. Which meant he wouldn't have time to do the drills with Alana. So he sent a message to Bishop, asking him to fill in. He sent Alana a message saying the same thing—no more, no less.

He happened to see Bishop the following day, and learned Alana had qualified on the phase pistol. He saw Phlox as well, and learned Alana hadn't spoken with him at all.

Give her time, he told himself.

He gave her two days. And then he buzzed her in her quarters.

"Lieutenant." Alana sounded surprised to hear from him.

"Ensign. I've just finished reading the Corbett." Which wasn't exactly the truth—he'd actually finished it several days ago, and it had lain next to his bunk that whole time. But it provided a convenient excuse now to talk to her. "I thought I might drop by and return it to you."

Alana was silent a moment. "I'm on day shift tomorrow—you can just leave it there, if it's easier."

"Actually, I wanted to talk to you as well. About Doctor Phlox," he added hurriedly. "Why you haven't been to see him."

"I didn't think it necessary."

"That's what I want to talk about."

"Sir, I think I can work this through on my own."

"I know you do. I—" Reed stopped, because he realized he'd forgotten to punch the button in on the com so she could hear what he was saying.

"Look," he said, pressing the button and starting over, "this is a silly way to have a conversation. Let me come talk to you—or we can meet in the mess hall."

More silence. "No. Here is fine."

"Good. I'll see you in five minutes. Reed out."

Reed closed the com, and picked up the Corbett. *You're making a mistake*, the little voice in his head whispered. *Going to her quarters.*

But he wasn't. He was her superior officer, and he had a responsibility to see that she was in optimum mental and physical health. And when Alana's door opened, and they both smiled on seeing each other, he knew he'd done the right thing.

"Here," he said, handing her the Corbett, and stepping inside. "And thank you."

"You're welcome." She set the book down behind her, next to a glass of water.

"I've been doing some thinking," she said. "And I've decided you're right. I need to get it off my chest—what happened on the *Achilles*."

"Excellent." Reed smiled. "So you'll call Phlox tomorrow?"

"No."

"I don't understand."

She looked at him then. "I want to talk to you about it, actually."

And all of a sudden that little voice was back.

It sounded like Captain Archer.

"Don't you get involved in playing counselor, Malcolm. Too much temptation to abuse your position as her superior officer. That's why we have those regulations, you know."

He pushed it to the back of his head.

"Of course," he said, pulling out a chair and sitting. "That's why I'm here."

"We were there to show the flag," Alana said. "Out near Arcturus. Just letting the colonies—and the pirates—know that Starfleet was still out there. Keeping an eye on things."

She was sitting on the edge of her bunk. Reed's

chair was pulled up next to her. It had taken them a while to work around to their subject—first he congratulated her on qualifying on the phase pistol, she asked him about the marker buoy, they talked about Bishop, and some of the other armory crew, and a whole lot of other things as well, managing, Reed noticed, to skip entirely over the fact that he'd been avoiding her for the last several days. Which he was glad of, because he felt stupid about it now. Acting like an idiot schoolboy of all things. He and Alana—he and Hart—were going to be fine. They were going to have a professional relationship, and be good friends as well, and that little voice in the back of his head was just plain wrong.

Alana had poured herself a drink—offered him one too, but he'd declined. She sipped from her glass now, and continued her story.

"Dinai Station—you know where it is, right? All the way out in Starfleet's patrol territory—the end of the line. We got there two months into our mission, and everything was fine. Stopped for a couple days, stretched our legs, and continued on our merry way. Two days later, though, we were back." She shook her head. "That's when everything went wrong."

"You went back to Dinai? I don't understand."

"It's so stupid," she said, standing up suddenly. "A gasket or something blew on the protein resequencer. We were low on everything, so we had to turn around. Get it fixed. When we returned—the pirates were there."

Reed shook his head. *Pirates*. The word seemed like such an anachronism here in the twenty-second century, but what else could you call them? He'd heard enough horror stories from Travis, who'd grown up on cargo ships, to know that they were real enough. And quite dangerous.

"They were probably stalking you the whole way," he said. "Waiting for *Achilles* to leave the station so they could move in, knowing you wouldn't be back for a long time."

"I suppose so," Hart said. "Only it didn't work out that way. As soon as we hailed the station, Captain Lyman knew something was wrong. They used a code word in responding. An SOS."

"So what'd you do?"

"Captain Lyman sent two of us in, from security—myself and Lieutenant Ayers, he was the head of our department. We pretended to be engineering staff, looking for the resequencer parts. Once we got down to the storage sheds, we were supposed to use the maintenance ducts to double back—surprise them. But the pirates had already gotten nervous. They had doubled the guard on the hostages. Put people on the ducts as well."

"So they got you too."

"Not me. Ayers, yes, but not me." She shook her head. "But after that—we lost the element of surprise. They were waiting for us. Captain Lyman tried to send in reinforcements, but—I don't know, it turned into a madhouse. When it was over, two of the hostages were dead. So was the captain, and five more of my crewmates. *Achilles* had a big hole in her side, and the pirates were gone, with all the dilithium."

Reed could only shake his head.

"What a disaster," he said finally. "I'm sorry that you had to go through that."

"Me? I lived," Hart said sharply. "Not a disaster for me."

"I still don't understand, though—why does Starfleet want what happened covered up?"

"Because," she said, draining her glass, "the hostages that died were Vulcans. And Starfleet weapons killed them."

"Dear God." Reed understood at last. The last hundred years of Vulcan policy were based on the assumption that mankind was too volatile a species to be allowed out into the wider galaxy. Only in the last decade or so had they relaxed enough to give humanity access to more of its technology, enough so that ships like *Enterprise* could be built, and sent out among the stars.

If what really happened at Dinai had been made public, odds were this ship would never have been launched.

"No wonder they didn't want you to say anything," Reed said. "Then, or now."

"Oh, it's even worse than that," Alana said. "I was the one who killed them."

Now Reed truly didn't know what to say.

"Everyone who worked at the station wore these orange coveralls. That was their uniform. So when—I came around one corridor and saw these two walking toward me, and I didn't see those uniforms—I fired." She drained the last of her glass. "With my trusty EM-33."

"Alana—"

"Compensated for the particle drift, and all. Hit them both dead-on. Thing was, though, the pirates were smart. They dressed the hostages up like bad guys, and used them as stalking horses. See," she shook her head, and poured herself another drink. "So you really can't tell anyone about this, you know. Not even the captain."

She raised the glass.

"Stop," he said. "That's an order."

She took a healthy swig, and set it down. "I'm off duty, sir."

He reached for the glass, intending to take it away from her. She reached at the same time. The glass tipped . . .

And spilled all over the Corbett.

"Christ, I'm sorry." There was a towel on the table—he grabbed it and started mopping up.

"Leave it," Alana said. "It's just a facsimile."

Her voice came from right behind him. He turned around, and she was inches away.

"This is real," she said, leaning forward. Her lips brushed his.

It was real.

It was wrong.

"Alana," he said, pushing away. "I want to, but—we can't. I'm sorry."

"Malcolm," she said. "It's a stupid regulation."

"But there it is," he said. "I'm a lieutenant. And you're an ensign."

"For now. Not always." She smiled. "If I've learned anything in my short awful career, it's that you never know what disaster tomorrow might bring. I mean, we're here right now. And beyond that . . ."

Reed felt for her. He wanted to take her in his arms.

"I can't have this conversation with you." He spun on his heel, and headed for the door.

"Wait. I'm sorry." She stood there, head bowed. "Please. Don't go away mad."

"I'm not mad," he said. "Not even close to it. I'm—" He waved his hands in frustration. "I don't even know what I am."

She smiled then—a bittersweet smile.

"I just wanted to say thank you—for listening. For everything."

"Of course," he said, and their eyes met, and Reed knew that if he stayed one second longer he was going to take her into his arms, and he wasn't going to stop with a kiss.

He left without looking back, wondering briefly why she had said thanks "for everything."

The mystery cleared when he woke the next morning and checked his computer for messages.

The first thing he found was a copy of Alana's transfer request.

Nine

"SUCH BEHAVIOR IS ILLOGICAL in the extreme."
T'Pol steepled her hands together on the table in
front of her. "The Sarkassians have antago-
nized and alienated Starfleet as well as its many
allies. Diplomatic relations will be affected for
years."

"It's the worst damn bit of ambassadoring I've
ever heard of," Trip said.

"Agreed," the captain said. "So why would she
do it?"

The *Enterprise*'s senior staff—Archer, Trip, T'Pol,
Reed, and Hoshi—were gathered around the table
in the captain's mess. Someone had brought in a
pot of coffee and a tray of sandwiches. Both sat
untouched in the middle of the table.

"Malcolm, Commodore Roan told you this was a religious war. Do you think—"

"No, sir." Reed shook his head. "I think the religious component of the war comes into play on the Ta'alaat side, not the Sarkassian. They seem far more pragmatic. This is the act of a—" He paused, searching for the right word.

"Fanatic?" Hoshi suggested.

"Exactly."

Archer shook his head. "So we come back to why again."

"Crime of passion?" Trip said after a moment. "He said something that got her so angry that she lost control for a moment?"

"So why not say that?" Archer replied.

Trip shrugged. "I don't know."

"Sir," Reed said, suddenly realizing something. "Why not say it even if it weren't true?"

"I don't follow," Hoshi said.

"I believe I do." T'Pol turned to Reed. "The lieutenant is suggesting that the ambassador's actions after the murder were intentionally inflammatory. That she could have at least attempted to minimize the effects of her crime."

"Exactly," Reed said.

"So the question becomes not so much why, as why *here?*"

The room fell silent.

"You're suggesting she intentionally sabotaged relations with Starfleet?" Archer said.

"We must consider the possibility," T'Pol said. "The ambassador indicated she acted on the orders of her government."

"Though we're not sure of that," Reed hastened to add. "Commodore Roan felt positive she wasn't."

"She was doing a pretty good job of pissing everybody off even before the murder, Captain," Trip said. "In a way, that was just the icing on the cake."

"Killing two birds with one stone," Archer said. "Get rid of Goridian, get us angry at the same time. Why, though? Why would they want to do that?"

"They do not want us around," T'Pol said.

Archer nodded. "Because of the outpost."

"That is the logical deduction. There is something down there they don't want us to see."

The captain frowned. "I don't know. What she did—that seems to me to have far worse consequences than any possible revelation."

"I would tend to agree with you, sir."

"Something else," Reed added. "Let's not forget that Goridian was the one who suggested the two of them talk. She may not have gotten the chance to do anything if not for him."

"That's right," Trip said. "And if you stop and look at it from that perspective, the one who really gains from us and the Sarkassians getting off on the wrong foot is Goridian and his people."

"Except he's dead," Archer said.

"Yeah." Trip threw up his hands. "Well, like I said, just another perspective."

"All right," Archer said, taking in everyone at the table with a look. "We need more information. About the war between these two people, about what exactly Ambassador Valay's orders were, and most especially about the outpost. Hoshi?"

"Aye, sir."

"I want you to get down to the lab and take a look at those new symbols Lieutenant Reed found."

"Yes, sir."

"T'Pol, you said the Vulcans haven't been out this far."

"That is correct."

"But they may have had contact with people who have—yes?"

"The possibility exists." She nodded. "I will conduct an extensive search of the database."

"Good. Malcolm?"

"Sir."

"Commodore Roan—he was going to contact you again?"

"He said he'd try."

"Let's be proactive," Archer said. "Perhaps you can contact him."

"The Sarkassians have refused all attempts at communication, sir," Hoshi cut in. "Lieutenant Reed and I tried to reach the commodore just before this meeting."

"Well, let's keep trying. Let's keep pushing. The

way things stand right now is not acceptable. Anyone has any ideas on how to change the status quo, find me. All right?" He looked around the table. "All right. Dismissed."

Reed stood and pushed his chair in.

"Lieutenant," the captain said. "Hold on a minute."

Archer waited until everyone else had left.

"Sit," he said.

Reed sat. So did the captain.

"Malcolm. Ensign Hart's autopsy results—"

"Yes, sir," Reed said, interrupting. "They're not ready yet. The doctor told me he would let me know as soon as they were."

"No. They are ready."

"Sir?"

"Doctor Phlox just transmitted them to me."

"Yes, sir." Reed kept his eyes straight ahead.

"Don't be mad at him. My orders. I wanted them before anyone else. I needed them." Archer shook his head. "Though I'm not sure I understand them any better than the doctor does."

Reed frowned. "Excuse me, sir?"

"Phlox says"—the captain hesitated—"that the cause of death appears to have been asphyxiation."

"What?" Reed wasn't sure he'd heard right.

"Asphyxiation—Ensign Hart simply stopped breathing."

"But why . . ."

"We don't know, Malcolm. The doctor did also

find considerable neurological disruption. It's possible that was the root cause."

"I see."

Archer sighed. "For what it's worth, he was able to confirm that the phase pistol was set on stun. She shouldn't have died, Malcolm."

"Yes, sir," Reed said, nodding tightly. "I know."

Except she had.

"I'm going to need to file a report with Starfleet," the captain said. "Which means I'll need your version of what happened."

"Yes, sir."

"I know there's a lot going on," Archer said. "But as soon as you can—"

"By tomorrow morning, sir. It'll be in the system."

"Good. I appreciate it." Archer hesitated. "One other thing, Malcolm. Just so you know—there's no question in my mind about the incident. I stand behind you one hundred percent."

"Thank you, sir."

"Which means I'm taking your word for something else, too."

"Sir?"

"That no matter what Doctor Phlox found—or didn't find—something happened to Ensign Hart down there. Something that made her behave the way she did. And we're going to get to the bottom of it."

"So we're not leaving yet?"

"Hell, no."

"Thank you, sir."

"Thank you," Archer said. "Listen. Try to get Roan one more time tonight. But if you can't—get some sleep. You look like you need it."

Reed smiled. "That is an understatement, Captain."

"All right, then." Archer stood up. "Dismissed."

The captain was right. He needed to sleep. The way his mind was racing, though . . . he wasn't sure he could. What he could do was eat—he hadn't had anything since breakfast.

The mess hall was practically deserted. Two crewmen from medical in the corner, laughing, heads bowed together over what looked like coffee and dessert. Fraternizing.

The regulations didn't apply to them. Not the way they had to him and Alana. It wasn't fair. It was blatantly unfair, in fact. Trip was right—those rules were going to change. Too late for him, though.

Reed picked out some leftover lasagna—vegetarian, he thought the chef said, though when he took his first few bites he could have sworn he tasted meat. Probably synthetic. He didn't care.

He picked at his food absently, thinking about Alana, about Goridian, and Valay, and Roan. What he'd seen down at the outpost. It was all tied together somehow, though he was too tired to even try to make the pieces fit.

Coffee then, he thought, and went and got a big mugful. Added milk—and sugar for good measure, which he never did. A little extra energy.

He set the mug back down on the table, and sat. One of the two crewmen from medical laughed, and spoke quietly to the other. He heard the sound of chairs pushing back, then footsteps. When he looked up, he was alone.

He stared at the empty chair across from him, and pictured Alana again, the night they met in her quarters, and talked about Dinai Station.

"Thing was, the pirates were smart," she said. "They dressed the hostages up like bad guys, and used them as stalking horses."

His vision swam for a second then—and in his mind, he saw her leaning forward, till her face was only inches apart from his, so close her features blurred.

"They dressed up," she repeated. "They weren't who they seemed to be. Do you understand?"

He didn't. He didn't remember her using those words.

"Malcolm," she repeated, leaning even closer. God, she was right there with him. "Listen to me."

I am listening, he said, almost to himself. *I am.*

But he was so tired.

He laid his head down on the table a second to rest.

Ten

"I CAN TELL YOU EXACTLY WHAT THE PROBLEM IS," Trip said from several feet above and to the right of Reed. "An excess of energy."

"Which is why we need to modify these circuits, not reroute them," Reed replied. He had one knee down on the deck, the front panel off the auxiliary control relays, and was busy tracing the energy flow from the plasma conduits to the firing circuits. "Reconfiguring the energy grid is the only way to make sure the system works as a unit."

Trip snorted audibly.

"Whoa, whoa. Hold on a minute there, mister."

Reed pinched a bundle of conduit between thumb and forefinger so as not to lose track of the line he was tracing, and looked up.

They were trying out the latest in a series of

modifications Reed had proposed for the ship's phase cannons. Neither man wanted a repeat of what had happened the last time they'd used those weapons—two full days of double shifts, repairing the overheated circuits.

Trip wagged the diagnostic caliper in his hand at Reed. "We are not goin' to reinvent the wheel here. There's no need for that—all we want is to maximize the energy output of this one component, of this one system. Besides . . ." He lowered his voice and leaned closer to Reed. "When I was talking about excess energy, I wasn't talkin' about the damn phase cannons, Malcolm." He smiled. "I was talking about you and Ensign Hart."

"Oh for God's sake," Reed said, standing up quickly. "You're not going to start in on that again, are you?"

Trip held up his hands in mock surrender. "Just trying to help out."

"Your concern is touching," Reed said. "But unnecessary."

"Why's that?" Trip asked.

"Ensign Hart is transferring," he said.

Trip's mouth fell open in surprise. "What?"

"Transferring," Reed said. "As in leaving the ship."

And with that, Reed turned and crossed the length of the armory to the far circuit panel, where the energy conduit from the engineering deck entered the room.

"Whoa, whoa, whoa," Trip said, catching up to him. "First of all, how can she transfer off *Enterprise?* We don't exactly make regular ports of call."

"The next cargo ship, transfer station, docking facility—the next nonhostile headed toward Earth, she'll be on it."

"Well . . . damn," Trip said. "Why?"

Reed flashed on Alana's face last night, when he'd stood in the doorway of her quarters and said goodbye.

"Malcolm?" Trip repeated. "Why?"

"You'd have to ask her," Reed said. "Excuse me."

He unscrewed the access panel, found the line that branched off to the cannon relays, and made sure the power to it was shut down. Which was harder to do than he thought it would be. It would be a good idea to have a convenient way to close that down without going into the interior workings of the system. A safety switch, for lack of a better term. He pulled out his padd from his back pocket and added that item to his to-do list.

He noted that Captain Archer had scheduled a meeting to discuss Alana's transfer request later that afternoon. He could see how that one was going to play out already.

"I didn't exactly abuse my position, sir," Reed heard himself saying.

Archer would nod, and not say anything for a moment. And then, "How—exactly—would you characterize what you did?" the captain would say.

And Reed pictured himself standing in the ready room, shuffling his feet, clearing his throat, and searching for the words to describe his actions of the past week and a half with regard to Alana.

Wonderful, he thought, snapping the padd shut. *I'm really looking forward to that.*

A dozen feet away, Bishop had the weapons locker open, and was checking charges on the phase pistols. He worked in silence, his movements practiced and precise.

"So what are you going to do about it?"

He looked up and saw Trip standing next to him again.

"About what?"

"Ensign Hart's transfer."

"What can I do? That's what she wants, I suppose."

"Is it?" Trip asked. "Ship's grapevine has it that her, and you—"

"Trip," Reed said, lowering his voice. "There are rules about officers fraternizing with subordinates, in case you hadn't heard."

"Rules," Trip snorted, following Malcolm over to the torpedo bays. "Bunch of pencil-pushers back in San Francisco copying over old Navy regulations into the Starfleet manual? That's a rule that needs to get changed, and quick."

"Those Navy regulations were put in place for good reason."

"Different times, my friend. How long you think we're gonna be out here? One year? Two?"

"At least," Reed said.

Trip nodded. "You got that right. I've heard rumors of five, and maybe even longer. And we're not always going to be near a starbase, or a planet like Risa. Besides, this is not your father's navy, am I right?" He prodded Malcolm with the caliper. "Things are going to happen. Those regulations are an anachronism. Mark my words, you'll not only be seeing relationships aboard starships, but weddings too."

"You might be right," Reed said. "But until the regulations change, it's our duty to obey them."

He bent down, then, and checked the energy flow from the conduit to the bays.

Trip bent down with him.

"You ought to speak to the captain. That's what I'd do. Tell him you and Ensign Hart—"

Reed had had enough.

"Trip, as far as I'm concerned, Ensign Hart is a closed subject—all right?"

The armory fell silent for a second.

Which was when Reed realized he'd spoken rather louder than he'd intended. Shouted, actually.

He looked around the armory, and saw Bishop staring at the two of them. Bishop saw him looking, and quickly turned back to his work.

Reed turned back to Trip.

"Sorry," he said. "I didn't mean to yell."

"I get your point, Malcolm," Trip said quietly. "I was only trying to be your friend here."

And he went off to the far corner of the armory to busy himself with something else.

Wonderful, Reed thought again. *Piss off the captain's number two, then piss off the man in charge. Good strategy. What a perfect day this is turning out to be.*

The armory door slid open, and Alana walked in.

Bishop and Trip both looked over at her, and promptly looked away.

Alana stopped in her tracks.

"Is something wrong?" Her gaze went around the room, and settled on Reed. She looked puzzled. Reed was puzzled too, but for a different reason.

"Ensign?" he said. "What—why are you here? You're not on till tonight."

She snapped to attention, then, her gaze focused on the wall directly behind Reed.

"I'm covering for Diaz. She's sick."

She wouldn't look at him. But Reed couldn't stop looking at her. At that instant, he wanted nothing more than to walk right over to her and tell her the transfer was stupid, and he was stupid, and the regulations were stupid, and the two of them should march hand-in-hand up to Captain Archer and tell him that in so many words.

"The regulations are stupid?" he pictured the captain saying.

"Yes, sir." He saw himself standing firm in front of the captain, sharing a smile with Alana.

In his mind, Archer turned to Hart. "Would you excuse us a second, Ensign?'

"Of course, sir."

And then she left the room, and Archer turned to Reed and said—

"Let's talk about stupid for a moment, all right, Malcolm?"

He shook his head, and returned to reality.

"All right, Ensign," Reed said to Alana. "Why don't you assist Mister Bishop with the phase pistols?"

"Yes, sir," she said.

Reed turned his back to the two of them and returned to work.

Perhaps thirty seconds later, he became aware of someone standing next to him.

He looked up to see Alana glaring at him.

"I would have preferred," she said through clenched teeth, "to tell my shipmates myself about the transfer."

"I'm sorry." Reed quickly stood. "The commander and I were having a private conversation, and we were overheard."

"Yes, sir," she said. "In the long run, I suppose it doesn't really matter."

"It does matter. And I apologize." He lowered his voice. "Alana, I wish you had come to talk to me before putting in this request."

"It's my decision, sir. I didn't see the need to talk to you about it."

"Alana." Reed lowered his voice. "You don't have to keep calling me sir."

"Of course I do," she said, her lips tight. "Regulations. Sir."

"Oh for God's sake." Reed shook his head. "This sort of conversation is exactly why—"

The com sounded. "Bridge to armory."

That was Captain Archer.

"Excuse me," he said to Alana, and walked over to the com panel.

"Armory. Lieutenant Reed. Go ahead, sir."

"We need you up here, Lieutenant. And if Commander Tucker's with you—"

"Right here, Captain," said Trip, stepping up next to Reed. The commander looked amused—Reed had no doubt Trip had been listening to his conversation with Alana.

"You'd better head over to engineering, Trip."

"What's up, Captain?" Trip asked.

"Hoshi's picked up something on subspace," Archer said. "I want everyone at their stations."

"Aye, sir," Reed said. "Out."

"We'll have to continue this project later, Lieutenant Reed," Trip said. There was a twinkle of amusement in his eye. "And our previous conversation as well."

And with that, he was out the door.

Reed turned back to Alana.

"Ensign, we'll have to finish our conversation later as well, I'm afraid."

"No need," she told him. "It's already finished. Sir."

She walked back over to the weapons locker, and started checking phase charges again.

Reed thought about saying something. But he couldn't think of what.

After a moment, he gave up and headed for the turbolift.

The bridge was a beehive of activity. Reed assumed his station, and pulled up a quick readout of the ship's tactical systems. All were at nominal status.

"Signal strength is increasing, Captain," Hoshi said. "But still very faint."

"Put it up on speakers, if you can," Archer said.

"Yes, sir."

A buzz of static filled the air. Reed couldn't make out anything intelligible through it.

"Can you clean it up?" Archer asked, swiveling in his chair toward Hoshi.

"Trying, sir," she said. Her hands flew across the control surface at her station. The static eased up a little bit. Syllables—nonsense, all of them, as far as Reed could tell—filled the bridge.

"The pattern is repeating—seven distinct fragments," Hoshi said. "It's a recording of some sort." She cocked her head to one side, her eyes half-closed, listening intently.

Reed tried to listen as well. The voice was pitched low—male, was his first guess—and whoever was speaking sounded quite anxious. Panicked, even.

"Sounds like a distress signal," the captain said, echoing his own thoughts.

Hoshi nodded. "Quite possibly, sir."

"May I remind you both," T'Pol said, "it is dangerous to project one culture's behavioral characteristics onto another."

"I know that," Hoshi said. "That's why I'm running it through the translation matrix."

Archer got up from his chair to stand by her station. He stood there a good five minutes. The bridge remained silent the whole time. Reed cleared the tactical status display from his monitor and brought up a sensor schematic of local space.

Finally, Hoshi shook her head. "Nothing, sir. Not enough to translate."

Archer nodded. "All right. We're going to proceed on the basis that it is a distress signal. Can we get a location on it?"

"I have been attempting to do just that," T'Pol said. She nodded toward the viewscreen, where the view of space outside the ship was suddenly replaced by a diagram.

"We have just entered the Eris Alpha system," T'Pol said. "A binary star system." The diagram showed two large dots right next to each other, surrounded by perhaps two dozen smaller ones at various distances. "Eris Alpha Prime is the larger star. The signal is coming from one of the planets nearest to it, or a point nearby. We'll need to drop out of warp to pinpoint its exact origin."

Archer nodded. "Bring us to impulse, Mister Mayweather."

The omnipresent thrum of the ship's warp engines died out, replaced by a much softer hum.

At her station, T'Pol was studying a number of readouts.

"Triangulating the transmission's source," T'Pol said. She studied the displays around her station, then looked up.

"There is a planetoid orbiting Eris Alpha III," she said. One of the smaller dots on the diagram filling the viewscreen began blinking. "That is the source of the transmission."

Archer took his chair again. "Take us there, Mister Mayweather. Full impulse."

"Aye, sir."

Reed tied in to the sensors, and began scanning the area they were heading toward. He whistled softly. "A lot of background radiation around that area, sir. No wonder the signal is so distorted."

"A lot of debris in the space surrounding the planetoid as well," T'Pol chimed in.

"Weapons fire?" Archer asked.

Reed exchanged a quick glance with T'Pol, and nodded. "Quite possibly, sir," Reed said. "The energy signatures are indicative of a number of small explosions—or a single larger one."

"How recent?"

"Very," T'Pol said. "Within the last twenty-four hours."

Reed had already reached the same conclusion from the readouts at his console. Now he keyed in a series of commands to his console that brought the armory crew to alert status.

Archer nodded. "How sophisticated is the technology involved? Are we talking about warp-capable species?"

"Impossible to tell from this distance," T'Pol answered.

"Any records in the Vulcan archives of civilizations out here?"

"Vulcans have not been out this far, sir."

"ETA, Travis?" Archer asked the helmsman.

"Thirty seconds, sir."

The time passed in silence. Reed alternated looking between his sensors and the viewscreen. A planet drifted into view—barren rock, a moon-desolate, crater-filled surface. As they circled it, they came up on a smaller body in orbit.

"The larger body is Eris Alpha Three, the smaller its moon," T'Pol said. "Neither contains an atmosphere. Several artificial structures—a number of them still intact—on the planetoid."

Reed was reading the same information off his monitor. He saw that the structures were divided into two basic types—roughly two dozen smaller ones, arranged in a series of rings around a handful of larger structures. The smaller ones were composed of a construction-grade titanium alloy, and the larger ones—

Hmm. That was odd.

"Life signs?" Archer asked.

"None," T'Pol replied. "But the radiation makes that reading less than a hundred percent certain."

Reed wondered if the radiation was affecting the readings he was getting as well. He tried to adjust the sensors to compensate, and failed. No change.

"How about that message, Hoshi?" Archer asked.

"Still receiving it, sir."

"There could be survivors down there." The captain looked around the bridge. "Yes?"

T'Pol nodded. "The possibility exists."

"I'd like to send down a landing party," Archer said.

"There are potentially hazardous radiation levels down there, sir," T'Pol said. "A number of areas we would have to avoid."

Reed cleared his throat. "Something else, sir. Some of those structures on the planet below—they simply don't scan."

"What do you mean?" Archer asked.

"The sensors don't pick them up at all. It's as if they don't exist."

"Confirming that, Captain," T'Pol said, looking up from her display. "Several buildings—as well as significant portions of the debris—appear to be composed of an alloy resistant to our sensors."

"How is that possible?" Archer asked.

"It's not," T'Pol said.

"I see. That's very interesting," Archer said. A smile tugged at the corners of his mouth.

Reed didn't share his commanding officer's excitement. Interesting had—more often that not, in his limited deep-space experience—proven to be dangerous.

"Let's find out if anyone's alive down there." Archer looked around the bridge. "Hoshi, you and I. Malcolm, and Commander Tucker. We'll rendezvous in launch bay one. Ten minutes."

Reed stepped forward. "If I might suggest, sir—additional security personnel?"

"Lieutenant Reed's suggestion is a good one, Captain," T'Pol added. "You could be walking into a combat zone."

"All right," Archer said. "Additional security personnel as you see fit, Mister Reed. Have them meet us at the shuttlepod."

Reed nodded. "Yes, sir."

The captain and Hoshi left the bridge. Reed sat at his station a moment, considering how to supplement the landing party. He wanted Bishop, for sure. And one other person. With so much ground to cover on the surface, they would most likely split the landing party into two smaller groups.

Reed brought the duty roster up on screen, and saw that Diaz was up in the rotation.

Except Diaz was sick. And Alana was covering for her.

Reed hesitated. Given the tension between them . . . it might be best to put someone else on the team.

On the other hand . . .

That wasn't about his level of comfort. It was about the job. And she was now fully qualified to do the job.

Bishop and Hart it was, then.

He opened a channel to the armory, and ordered them both to report to the shuttlebay.

Eleven

MESS HALL
1/17/2151 04:31 HOURS

"LIEUTENANT REED."

His eyes snapped open. For a second, he was totally disoriented. Then he looked up and saw Dr. Phlox standing over him.

"Good Lord." Reed sat up and blinked. He'd passed out at the mess hall table. On the table, to be more precise. "What time is it?"

"Ship's time is four-thirty. In the morning."

"Oooh." He stretched, and yawned, and blinked again. "I fell asleep."

"That much is clear." Phlox smiled. "May I suggest using your bunk for that purpose in the future?"

"Expert medical advice, Doctor. I'll try and follow it." Reed massaged the back of his neck. "What are you doing up at this hour?"

"I had trouble sleeping. I have been considering the matter of Ensign Hart's death."

Reed was suddenly wide awake.

"And?"

"I understand the captain shared the autopsy results with you?"

"He summarized them for me, yes."

"I am not entirely pleased with my findings." Phlox pulled out the chair next to Reed. "May I?"

"Of course."

The doctor sat. "When you first brought Ensign Hart back to the ship, you'll recall I took a series of readings in sickbay."

"I remember. Yes."

"Then you may also recall those test results were inconsistent with ones I'd taken earlier, while giving Ensign Hart her initial shipboard physical."

"I remember," Reed said, rubbing his eyes again. He didn't see where Phlox was going with this. "Go on, Doctor."

"Of course you do." Phlox nodded. "Well. To continue. After making the appropriate correlations, I—" He looked at Reed more closely, and his voice trailed off. "I am being inconsiderate, Lieutenant. You have had little sleep and, I suspect, little to eat over the last few days."

"It's not important," Reed said.

"Ah." Phlox shook his head. "Sustenance is always important. Maintenance of the body's internal combustion engine, as it were. Essential to proper brain function. You should have breakfast, Lieutenant. I have asked the staff to prepare for me a frittata—have you ever had one? It is an egg dish not unlike an omelette, filled with vegetables and all manner of meat products."

"Meat products?" Reed's stomach rolled over at the thought. "No, no. I'll grab something later."

Phlox frowned. "I must insist you eat something, Lieutenant."

"Doctor . . ."

"Lieutenant, one of my most important duties as chief medical officer is to insure that every person in this crew is in optimum physical and mental condition, fully capable of fulfilling the demanding schedule required of him and or her as a member of—"

"Doctor, I'm fine," Reed protested.

"Required of him and or her," Phlox went on, ignoring the interruption, "as a member of Starfleet. Now. I know for a fact that you have had very little sleep these last few days, and I would be remiss in performing my job if I did not—"

"All right, all right." Reed held up his hands in surrender. "Toast, then. With jam. And coffee."

"Excellent. Excuse me a moment, and I will place your order." Phlox rose from his chair and went over to talk to the chef. A moment later he returned with two plates—his significantly larger than the one he passed to Reed. One of the kitchen staff came by with coffee for both of them.

"To continue," Phlox said, between bites. "Or rather, to summarize my concerns. The correlations between Ensign Hart's earlier readings, from the *Achilles,* and the ones I took at the time she returned to the ship. There is none."

Reed, in the middle of sipping his coffee, frowned. "No correlation? What does that mean?"

The doctor shook his head. "I have absolutely no idea."

"Excuse me?" Reed couldn't believe he'd heard Phlox correctly.

"I can think of no explanation for the lack of correlation between these two sets of readings. They are a measurement of specific energy patterns that remain virtually unchanged over the lifetime of an individual. For them to be anything but identical . . ." he shook his head. "It is impossible. As if I had been examining two different patients."

Reed had never heard Phlox sound so perplexed. He thought a moment. "Could these readings explain why she behaved as she did? So out of character?"

"Possibly." The doctor shrugged. "Though again, for all I know, her actions could just as easily be accounted for by a chemical imbalance, psychological stress . . ."

"Wonderful," Reed said, wondering if what he'd put her through—their on-again, off-again relationship—could have had anything to do with what had happened to her later.

"Lieutenant? Is something the matter?"

Reed looked up to see Phlox studying him carefully.

"Not really. Just wondering if anything I did might have contributed to a breakdown."

"I'm sure your actions were not a source of stress for Ensign Hart."

"Yes, well . . ." Reed sighed. "It's a complicated issue, Doctor."

"I understand. Your relationship with Ensign Hart had nothing to do with what happened to her, Lieutenant. I can assure you of that."

Phlox smiled. Reed felt himself flush. "Relationship. What—"

"Lieutenant. There is no need to dissemble with me."

For a second, Reed was puzzled. It sounded like Alana had been confiding in Phlox as well.

Then he realized she probably had.

"She talked to you about all this."

"Ah." The Doctor allowed himself a small smile. "I must assert doctor–patient privilege, Lieutenant. However . . . I can tell you that after composing her transfer request, the ensign did have cause to stop by my office. And I can state categorically that whether or not she would have ended up serving here aboard *Enterprise*, or elsewhere—Ensign Hart was in a far better position to deal with whatever came her way because of your relationship."

"Really?" Reed felt a smile tugging at the corners of his mouth.

"If you'll permit me a few observations." The doctor went on without waiting for a reply. "Being forced to keep secret what happened aboard the *Achilles*—it took a toll on her, that to a large extent, she lost the ability to confide in people. She became afraid to trust, afraid to form relationships. Her friendship with you was, I believe, a very important step forward in terms of her mental well-being. The connection you made helped her begin to deal with her feelings. Up until that point, the guilt and regret she felt had, in a very real sense, paralyzed her development."

Reed didn't know what to say to all that. He was glad that he'd been able to help Alana, but at the same time . . .

"Lieutenant. Guilt and regret. Ensign Hart lived with them for years, and they were not kind companions." Phlox leaned forward, across the table. "Do you understand what I'm saying?"

Reed met the doctor's eyes, and saw the concern there.

Phlox was talking about him, he realized—about the guilt that he felt over what happened to Alana. And Reed wondered, suddenly, if the Doctor hadn't come looking for him this morning specifically to have this conversation.

"Ensign Hart was able to find a sympathetic ear in you," Phlox said. "I'm sure many in the crew would have appreciated the opportunity to help her. Would have considered it a privilege to serve as such a—a sounding board, I believe is the term."

"Yes." Reed replied. "That's the term."

"I thought so. To my point again—many in the crew would be happy to serve as such a sounding board for any of their fellow shipmates in need. If you catch my meaning."

Reed nodded. "I do. Thank you, Doctor."

"Good." Phlox stood. "And now I must return to sickbay. If I am to append anything to my autopsy notes, it must be soon. Enjoy your breakfast."

"I will. Thank you, Doctor."

"You're very welcome."

He watched Phlox go, and realized the doctor was right. He should talk to someone about what had happened. He would find Trip, or perhaps the captain. Maybe even go back to Phlox. But for right now . . .

He had work to do. Thinking about the Doctor reminded him of the autopsy, and the fact that he'd promised the captain his report this morning, the report of what happened in the armory. *Do that now,* he thought, *and then grab a few more hours of sleep.* He took another bite of his toast, and stood up from the table.

Suddenly he realized he was starving.

Reed sat back down and had a full breakfast before leaving for his quarters.

He wrote his report for the captain, forcing himself not to linger on the details. After he sent it off, he undressed and took a long hot shower. Hot as he could stand it. He stood in the spray far longer than necessary, letting the water wash over his face and body without moving, without thinking, in a kind of numb, half-asleep state. He thought about Phlox, and the puzzling readings the doctor couldn't explain. The explanations for Alana's behavior they might never find.

Images flashed in his mind, as if someone had suddenly turned on a slide projector. Random snapshots from the last few days, pieces of a puzzle thrown up in the air and landing haphazardly.

Valay and Goridian arguing—and the ambassador's crown, dripping with blood.

Phlox, leaning over Alana's body in the armory.

Goridian in his cell, smiling as he assured the captain that he had nothing to do with what had happened to Ensign Hart.

And Alana—alive again, sitting behind him in the shuttlepod, as they sped toward the ruins of the Sarkassian outpost.

Twelve

THEY WERE FIVE MINUTES OUT from *Enterprise*, five minutes away from the outpost. Trip had the helm. Archer and Hoshi were in the jump seats immediately behind him, Bishop and Reed in the next row, and behind them, Alana, who had perfected the art of ignoring him. All were dressed in environmental suits, with their helmets off.

"Fifty kilometers," Trip said. "Maneuvering thrusters."

Archer, working one of the shuttlepod stations, nodded. "Online."

"Here we go." Trip switched off the impulse engines, and Reed felt a gentle boost of acceleration as the planetoid's gravity took hold of them, and the shuttlepod's engines fought back.

Reed had tactical sensors online, tied in to the *Enterprise*'s systems. Space all around them was clear. They were still picking up the distress signal. He'd narrowed down its source to the south end of the complex. There were also energy signatures coming from the north end, where the destruction appeared to be heaviest. Much of the debris was composed of that alloy their sensors were having trouble analyzing. Reed wanted to bring some of it back with them. He told the captain as much.

"I'd rather wait on that kind of thing, Lieutenant," Archer said. "At least until we know a little more about the situation. Think about how we'd feel if someone started carting off pieces of *Enterprise* after a battle."

"And if whoever built this station ends up being an adversary?" Reed said. "Think about the strategic advantage a material we can't detect gives them. Sir, with all due respect, I think this is one of those situations where we need to act in our own self-interest."

"I will think about it, Lieutenant," Archer said, working his station. "For the moment, let's leave everything where it is, all right?"

"Yes, sir," Reed said.

The captain's decision notwithstanding, he'd already put a few small sample containers into the side pockets of his environmental suit. Just in case Archer changed his mind.

Reed swung the sensor panel up and to the side of his seat. As he did so, he caught a glimpse of Alana in the seat behind him. She seemed calm enough. Ignoring him probably gave her something to focus on. He supposed that was a good thing.

He leaned forward and concentrated on what he could see through the shuttle's front window. The outpost was just coming into view—a splotch of gray against the reddish brown, rocky planetoid below. As they drew closer, he began to pick out individual structures—three larger ones (the smallest of which, on a rise at the very center of the complex, was shaped like a pyramid) surrounded by a handful of much smaller buildings. Debris was scattered everywhere, with much of it concentrated at the northern end of the complex. It looked to Reed as if there had been an explosion there—huge swatches of ground were burned black, and even from a distance he could make out several piles of twisted, gleaming metal.

"Over there, to the left," Archer said. "Looks like a landing field."

Reed had a bad angle. He couldn't see what the captain was talking about.

Trip could.

"I think you're right," the commander said. "You want to go around again, or set down now?"

"Let's get on the ground," Archer said. "See about that distress signal."

The shuttle banked to the left, and began descending. Reed got a better view of the pyramid-shaped building, but only for a moment. It looked like it was carved from a single piece of metal—possibly even stone. A narrow platform circled its base, with a long flight of steps leading up to it. He had no frame of reference to judge the pyramid's size, no way to judge how big those steps were or who they might have been designed for.

Wait. Yes, he did.

Reed swung the sensor panel back down in front of him, and brought it online.

Nothing. The pyramid was composed of that alloy the sensors couldn't pick up.

With a barely noticeable thump, the shuttle touched down. Reed pushed the sensor panel back up and out of the way, and stood.

"All right, everyone, you know your groups," Captain Archer said. He stood at the front of the shuttle, holding his helmet in one hand before him. "Hoshi and I are going to check out the distress signal at the south end of the complex. Trip, you go north to see what's giving off those strange energy signatures. Ensign Hart, Mister Bishop, you're with me. Malcolm, you're with Commander Tucker."

"Keep on eye on radiation levels," Trip added. "We don't know exactly what blew up down here, or what sort of particles might still be floating around."

"Security checks every five minutes," Reed added.

With those words, everyone began suiting up. Reed put on his helmet and activated the seal. Oxygen began flowing, and he wrinkled his nose. There was something about the smell of recycled air from a tank ... he'd never been able to get Trip to satisfactorily explain to him why *Enterprise*'s air didn't smell the same way.

He shuddered, and caught a glimpse of Alana as she sealed her helmet. She was making the same face.

He smiled.

"I don't know that I'll ever get used to that smell," he said.

"Yes, sir," she said, her face gone suddenly blank. She followed Trip out of the shuttle.

So much for small talk, Reed thought.

The planetoid's surface was as barren as Earth's moon—rocky and inhospitable. From orbit, it had a reddish orange color, but down this close, those shades all faded into a continuum of brown. There was a fine haze of dust swirling through the air.

It took Trip and Reed less than five minutes to reach the first of the smaller buildings. Except that as they got closer, Reed realized that they weren't buildings at all.

"These were ships," he said. "Fusion engines, minimal crew compartment—"

"Yeah." Trip, out in front, was the first to reach one. He stood next to it and looked up. "Reminds me of the old lunar modules, you know? The ones the Apollo astronauts used?"

Reed nodded. *Module* was a good word for what they were looking at. The structure resembled nothing so much as a cube, perhaps twenty feet tall and just as wide around, with appendages of various lengths and thicknesses sticking out of it. The appendages looked functional; Reed guessed they had served various communications and sensory purposes at one point.

"They flew them down, set 'em in place, and left 'em. Not too long ago, either." Trip ran a hand along the side of the module. "Look at the pitting on the surface here. I'd say a year."

"Not even that," Reed said. "Six months, at the most."

He pulled out his tricorder and took readings.

"Standard duranium/titanium composition, fairly recent construction."

"Malcolm." Reed turned and saw Trip standing by the next closest module, motioning to him. "Over here."

Reed put away his tricorder and approached the module. As he got closer, he saw something lying on the ground at Trip's feet. At first he thought it was one of the metal appendages from the module.

Three meters away, he realized it was a body.

Humanoid, but that was about all you could tell by looking at it. Whoever it was—had been—was not wearing an environmental suit. The body lay crumpled against the base of the module, buried up to its waist by the planetoid's drifting sand.

"What a mess," Trip said.

Reed bent down next to it, his tricorder still on.

"Not human," he said, studying the readings. "Thinner bones, slightly different skeletal structure—"

Trip shook his head. "I wonder what made him decide to take a walk without a spacesuit."

"Maybe he didn't." Reed adjusted the controls on the tricorder and frowned. "Look where the body struck the base. See that?"

"Yeah," Trip said. There was a slight discoloration there. "Blood, you think?"

"I do. And the skull is caved in at the back of the head as well."

"He fell?"

"No. The fracture is too severe to have been caused by a fall. I think he was thrown."

"By what?"

Reed stood up then, and looked around the outpost.

"I'm not sure."

Trip stood and looked around too. "Hey, hold on a minute. This whole thing—the modules in a circle—could have been a containment field here."

"Some kind of pressurized atmosphere?" Reed nodded. "That makes sense. It's the simplest explanation for why our spacesuited friend was walking around without a suit."

"Explosive decompression on that scale . . ." Trip bent down next to the module, and dug away at the base. "These things are in pretty deep—that's why they stayed put," he said a few seconds later, "but anything else—"

"Went flying," Reed finished. He looked around at the other modules, arranged in a circle, and nodded. "It could be. Some sort of field generator—"

"Or a field generator holding a layer of monofilament in place."

"Like a big tent," Reed said.

"Balloon is the image you're looking for," Trip said. "And somebody popped it."

"On purpose?"

"Let's look around a little more, see if we can find out," Trip said.

They made a circle around the larger building, checking out two more of the modules. Along the way they found another body, in much the same condition as the first. Again, not wearing a spacesuit of any kind.

Trip also found, sticking up out of the ground like a spear, one of the metal appendages from a module. Attached to it was a thin sheet of transparent material.

"Monofilament," Trip said, rubbing it between

his gloved fingers. It crumpled and flew away like the strands of a spider's web. "There was some kind of atmospheric containment field working here."

He reached up and flicked on his com switch.

"Tucker to Captain Archer."

"Archer here. Go ahead."

"Found something interesting, Captain." Trip proceeded to tell him about the bodies and the containment field.

Archer was silent a moment.

"Sir?" Trip prompted.

"We found bodies too," the captain said finally. "Four of them. Shot with some kind of particle weapon. Two in the back."

Everyone was silent a moment.

"Dead how long?" Reed asked, switching on his own com.

Bishop spoke up. "Best guess two days, sir." He described the dead aliens.

"Sounds like they belong to the same race as the ones we found," Trip said. "So I think we can take it as a given this place was attacked."

"Captain," Reed said. "I'd like to suggest that you, Commander Tucker, and Hoshi return to the ship. Let me bring down a full security team and reconnoiter before we do any further exploration."

"Whoever attacked the outpost seems to be gone," Archer said. "We're not picking up any life signs. And we are closing in on the source of the distress signal. If there are survivors, they could be in need of our help."

"Sir—"

"Your concern is noted, Lieutenant. And appreciated. Keep me posted on what you find, Commander."

"And you do the same," Trip replied. "Tucker out." He switched off his com.

"Commander," Reed said, allowing a touch of irritation to creep into his voice. "I really don't think it's a good idea for the captain to put himself into this kind of situation."

"I've had that conversation with him too, Malcolm. And I lost, same as you did."

"It's not prudent."

"Prudent, hell. It's dangerous. But he's the captain." Trip smiled. "End of story. You can bring it up again when we get back to the ship, if you want. For all the good it'll do you. But for now . . ." Trip looked down at his tricorder, then back up again. "I've got a fix on those energy readings you picked up from the shuttle." He pointed at the large building in the center of the complex. "There. Come on."

They set off again. As they walked, Reed deliberately fell back, and switched on his com again, this time to a private channel.

"Ensign Hart, do you read me?" he said quietly.

"Right here, sir."

"Mister Bishop's on point?"

"Yes, sir. I'm trailing."

"Good," Reed said. "I'm going to ask you to turn your tricorder on to maximum sensitivity, and keep a close eye on it."

"What am I looking for, sir? Other life signs?"

"No, Bishop will have his instruments set to read those things. I want you to be watching for any signs of increased radiation or structural flaws in the modules. This whole place has just gone through a series of very devastating events."

"Yes, sir. I'm setting the tricorder now."

"Anything you pick up—anything out of the ordinary—you call me. Is that understood?"

"Yes, sir."

Reed heard irritation in her voice.

"I'm not baby-sitting you, Ensign."

"No, sir."

The irritation was still there.

"Alana, I have no doubt you can do your job. It's just that keeping charge of the captain is something I take rather personally on these missions."

"Yes, sir." She still didn't sound mollified.

Reed didn't have time to try and explain himself further.

"I'll check in with you again shortly. Out."

He caught up with Trip just in time to examine the next module. They found nothing new there, no clues as to what might have happened to the containment field, or who attacked the outpost.

Nor did they find anything at the remaining three modules that formed the perimeter.

As they approached the larger building at the center of the complex, though, Reed noticed a number of shallow depressions in the ground off to his left—rectangular-shaped, perhaps two dozen feet on one side, half again on the other.

He stopped in his tracks. They reminded him, suddenly, of something—though for the life of him he couldn't remember what.

"Hold on, Commander," he called, taking out his tricorder. "What do you make of those?"

Trip turned around, and looked where he was pointing. "Man-made, for sure. Or alien-made, if you want to be a stickler about it."

"Tricorder says they go down about ten feet—to a level surface." Reed shook his head. "So what are they?"

"Somethin' we'll figure out later," Trip said. He started walking again. "Come on, Malcolm. The sooner we do this, the sooner we get the captain back to the ship safe and sound."

"All right," Reed said. But he stayed behind a moment longer, racking his brain for the memory that was eluding him. Finally, with a last shake of his head, he gave up and joined Trip again.

As they approached the building at the center of the complex, Reed could see that what he had earlier mistaken for a single, monolithic structure was in fact composed of two pieces—a rectangle on top, with a square base supporting it. Only it wasn't exactly a rectangle, nor exactly a square. The proportions were off—distorted.

Very strange. Very alien. And more than anything else, he thought, very, very old.

"Damn." Trip had his tricorder out and was shaking his head. "It's like a hundred-foot hole in the sensor readings. I'm not picking it up at all."

"It's the same alloy," Reed said absently, more focused on the building before him than what Trip was saying. The lieutenant was next to the base now; it extended about a dozen feet off the ground, and was composed of a single, polished surface. Metal, or stone—he still couldn't really tell. He couldn't see a crack in it, or a sign of stress anywhere. He raised a glove to touch it—

And jumped back in surprise.

"There's some kind of energy field around it."

"Low-level magnetic field," Trip said, walking up next to him and running his hand next to the base. "I feel it too."

The com crackled in his ear.

"Archer to Tucker."

"Go ahead, sir," Trip said.

"We found the transmitter. A communications device in one of the smaller modules, set to continuous broadcast. No sign of any survivors. We have found something else, though. A passageway, leading down. We're going to check it out."

Reed didn't like the sound of that.

"Sir—"

"I understand your concern, Lieutenant. Ensign Hart has suggested we leave a channel open so you can monitor what we're doing."

"Good suggestion," Trip said.

It was at that, Reed had to admit.

"Where are you, Trip?" the captain asked.

"Right at the source of those energy readings. One of the big buildings. But I don't see any way in to find out what's generating all this power."

"Well . . . find out what you can, and head back to the shuttle. We'll meet you there shortly."

"Aye, sir. Tucker out." He looked at Reed. "I'm gonna go check around the other side of the building."

"All right. Stay alert." Reed opened his own com. "Ensign Hart?"

"Right here, sir," Alana replied.

"I'll be on the channel we used previously."

"Yes, sir. Switching to monitor—now."

Reed listened. He heard breathing. Walking. Steps down a hard-floored passageway.

"Tell me what you're seeing, Ensign," he said.

"Not much. No ambient light. The passageway is about half as wide as the corridors aboard ship—roughly the same height. Composed of . . ." She paused. "Tricorder says mostly silicon."

Reed tried to remember what he knew about silicon. Lightweight. A very efficient energy conductor. He had never heard of it being used as a construction material.

"We're headed in your direction," Hart said. "The passageway appears to end—" The signal crackled. "—hundred feet."

"I missed part of that," Reed said. "You're breaking up."

"We're getting interference. I think from—" The crackle came again. "—near you."

"Boost your signal, Ensign."

"Aye, sir." Her voice suddenly came in much louder. "Better?"

"Much. Repeat that last part of your message."

"The interference is coming from the power source near you."

"That's not good."

"No, sir. Heading in your direction, the interference is likely to get worse."

As if on cue, the com crackled again.

Reed thought about telling Hart to ask the captain to turn back. He suspected he knew what kind of response she'd get.

"Malcolm!"

That was Trip, cutting in on the com. Reed turned and saw him waving.

"On the other side of the building—there's an opening. A door."

Reed waved back. "All right, Ensign," he said to Hart over the com. "I'll continue to monitor you. Out."

Reed came around the building. Trip stood next to the base, where a portion of the wall was simply missing. Or at least it looked that way at first.

Then Reed looked closer, and saw that part of the base was actually a door that had slid open to one side. Or been forced—the base next to it was blackened in spots, though otherwise undamaged.

"I went in about ten feet," Trip said. "There are steps, leading down. Into a passageway that sounds a lot like what the captain found."

"There may be a whole network of tunnels here, connecting the buildings. That would make sense."

Trip flipped on his com. "Tucker to Archer."

"Right here, Trip."

There was a lot of static on that channel too.

"You're breaking up, sir," Trip said. "Let's try another channel."

"Won't do any good," Reed cut in. "That's interference from the power source we picked up." He was also listening to the channel Ensign Hart had left open—now that was filled with static as well, though he could still hear sounds of the captain's party, moving forward.

Trip nodded. "Captain, looks like we've found the same kind of passage you did. Leading down."

"Well, we're headed in your general direction. Maybe we'll hook up."

"Maybe we will. Tucker out."

Each environmental suit had two lights, one on

either side of the helmet. Trip switched on his now. "You up for a little exploring?" he asked.

"On one condition." Reed snapped his tricorder shut, and slid it back in his pocket. Then he switched on his helmet lights. "I go first." Reed drew his phase pistol, and stepped forward into the tunnel opening.

Thirteen

THE COM SOUNDED, or Reed felt sure he might have fallen asleep on his feet in the shower, with the water still pounding on his back.

"Bridge to Lieutenant Reed."

He stepped out of the stall, and the water automatically shut off. He grabbed for a towel and the com at the same time.

"This is Reed. Go ahead."

"Good morning, Lieutenant. The captain requests your presence in the situation room immediately."

That was Travis—Ensign Mayweather. Reed checked the time on his monitor and saw that there was still almost two hours before his shift started.

"What's it about?"

149

"Don't know. But he got me up early to cover for O'Neil. She's going to be there. All the senior officers as well."

O'Neil was Lieutenant Donna O'Neil. D.O., everyone called her. She was the duty officer on third shift—night watch on the bridge. Her presence there told Reed that whatever the meeting was about, it had something to do with events that had taken place during her shift.

"Huh," Reed said, wondering what that something was. "Thanks, Travis."

"You're welcome."

"So you're the duty officer now? Alone on the bridge?"

"That's right."

"Stay out of the chair."

"Very funny. Bridge out."

Reed smiled. He'd caught Travis in the captain's chair once, early on in their mission, and had never let him forget about it. Tweaked him every chance he could. Mayweather took it well—no surprise there. He was a good kid—had the makings of a fine officer. A little excitable, perhaps, but then what young ensign wasn't?

Alana, he thought. She wasn't.

Reed finished getting dressed and reported to the situation room—which was really not a room at all, but a separate area at the rear of the bridge. Archer, Trip, Hoshi, and O'Neil were already there.

"Malcolm," the captain said, greeting him. Then Archer turned to O'Neil. "T'Pol's coming?"

"Yes, sir," the lieutenant said. "She's just completing an analysis of that interference."

Reed assumed O'Neil was talking about the trouble they were having with sensors. He wondered why T'Pol was worrying about that now.

"All right. We can get started without her. Most of this she already knows, anyway." Archer looked around the table. "Sorry to get everyone up so early. But as you'll see, I think the situation warrants it. D.O.?"

"Thank you, sir," O'Neil said. "Approximately forty-five minutes ago, we detected small-arms fire at the Sarkassian outpost. Roughly comparable in energy output to a series of bursts from our phase pistols. We believe a battle of some sort was taking place. Again, our sensor readings are not entirely reliable, but we feel almost certain there were several fatalities associated with this battle."

"Goridian had friends," Reed said. "They attacked the Sarkassians."

"That was my first thought too," Archer said. "Then we saw this."

While he spoke, O'Neil had gotten out of her seat and gone to the computer station at the far end of the room. She turned the monitor now so it was visible to everyone.

"During the battle, we intercepted the following

transmission," she said. "We've cleaned up the signal as much as possible, but it's still . . . well, you'll see."

She pressed a series of buttons. Static filled the air, punctuated by louder bursts of distorted speech. The screen went from black to a snowy, distorted gray. Then suddenly an image came into focus.

Commodore Roan was looking anxiously into the lens of whatever was transmitting his signal. Smoke filled the air behind him. Reed heard the sound of crying.

The commodore's robe—the same one he'd been wearing yesterday evening, during his visit to *Enterprise*, Reed noticed—was covered in blood.

". . . to Central Council. Roan to Central Council, do you read? I do not know why you have failed to respond to my previous message, but—"

The sound faded away into static again. The picture blurred, and then disappeared altogether. Reed looked at Archer.

The captain held up a finger. "Wait," he said.

Roan's image reappeared on the screen.

"—two are dead and the rest of us have approximately an hour's worth of breathable atmosphere in our—" The sound drifted into nothingness, then suddenly returned. "—ambassador refused to acknowledge our surrender or your—"

Static again. The screen faded to black.

O'Neil pressed the keypad again, and the room fell silent.

"That's it," Archer said.

Reed looked around the table. The others wore the same expression of surprise—bordering on shock, in some cases—he was sure he had on his face.

"How I read that," Reed said slowly, "is that the fight we detected was between Roan and Valay, and forces loyal to each of them."

"That's the only way to read it," the captain said.

"That's messed up," Trip said. "What is going on down there? Some kind of civil war?"

"Possibly. Or just more of what was going on while they were here. The tension between those two wasn't hard to miss."

"Tension is one thing. That down there . . ." Trip shook his head. "That's something else altogether."

"The question is, what do we do about it?" The captain looked around the table. "I'd like to hear your thoughts."

"You heard the commodore, sir," Reed said. "In his message, Roan said they had an hour's worth of breathable air. That was forty-five minutes ago."

"Approximately an hour's worth, he said," Trip pointed out.

"That leaves him with less than a quarter of an hour." Reed looked around the table. "Sir, we have to rescue him."

"That's one option," Archer said.

The turbolift hissed open, and T'Pol walked in. Archer waved her over.

"You're just in time, Sub-Commander. We were discussing Roan's message, and what to do about it."

"Rescue, sir," Reed said again. "We can't let the commodore die down there."

"My heart's with you on that, Lieutenant, but . . ." Trip frowned. "My head tells me we don't want to get involved in any sort of civil war here."

"Perhaps we could contact the Sarkassian government directly," Hoshi suggested. "Find out who's telling the truth."

"I know who I'd place my money on," Reed said.

"Contacting the Sarkassian government is an intrusive act in and of itself," T'Pol said. "We place ourselves squarely in the middle of the conflict by doing that."

"I have to disagree, Sub-Commander," Reed shot back. "We wouldn't be committing ourselves to any course of action. We'd just be trying to find out the truth."

T'Pol regarded him curiously. "Lieutenant. I suggest you consider the issue more thoroughly."

Reed hated it when she patronized him like that. "I am considering the issue. And I suggest to you there's a difference between physically interfering and simply asking questions."

"Lieutenant, by posing those questions to the

government we alter the situation whose objective truth we are trying to ascertain."

"You're getting a little too theoretical for me now," Reed said.

"This entire discussion is theoretical. We cannot contact the Sarkassian government."

"Why not?"

"Because of the jamming beam."

"What?" Hoshi looked even more surprised to hear that than she had after watching Roan's transmission. "We didn't pick up any kind of jamming beam before."

"It was not active until very recently. Some point within the last five-point-six hours, according to a log of our sensor readings."

"Back up a second," Archer said. "We can't contact the Sarkassians at all?" For the first time, he looked surprised.

So did O'Neil.

"I thought the jamming was specific to the frequency Roan was using," she said.

"As did I initially," T'Pol said. "But in completing my analysis of the beam, I discovered that the jamming appears to be transmission sensitive— that is, the Sarkassians have developed a device which actively scans the EM spectrum, searching for the presence of energy which has an artificially repetitive character to it. Such patterns do not, as a rule, occur in nature, and can thus be assumed to be indicative of artificially modulated energy. When it finds such a transmission, the device generates a mirror image of the wave it detects and sums it with the original, resulting in a null signal."

"Did you find out where the beam is originating from?"

"There is a small Sarkassian ship in geosynchronous orbit with the outpost. I believe that to be the source."

"We've got to take that beam out," Reed said.

"And how would you suggest we do that, Lieutenant?" T'Pol said.

Reed smiled. "We have a variety of options at our fingertips. Photon torpedoes, phase cannon, plasma charges." He smiled. "A good old-fashioned threat might do the trick."

T'Pol raised an eyebrow. "Lieutenant. Even you must admit that using our weapons on a Sarkassian ship would be an intrusive act."

"Of course it's an intrusive act," Reed replied. "How would you characterize what they're doing?"

"Securing their space."

"Excuse me?"

"We are in their territory." T'Pol said. "Furthermore—"

"That doesn't give them the right to jam our transmissions!"

"Furthermore," T'Pol continued. "Let us take stock of our situation at this instant in time. Deep in virtually unknown space, unable to communicate with the rest of Starfleet, and surrounded by hostile ships."

Reed sighed. He knew T'Pol was right, but . . .

"I understand your frustration, Lieutenant," Archer said. "But we can't just shoot them."

"Yes, sir."

"So what do we do about Roan, Captain?" Trip asked. "Because if we wait much longer, we won't have a decision to make there. His air will be gone."

"I'm well aware of our time frame, Commander," Archer said. He turned to O'Neil. "Do we know where the commodore was transmitting from?"

O'Neil nodded. "We can pinpoint his location fairly closely."

"Well, we can't exactly send down a shuttle to rescue him," Trip said. "I don't think the ambassador and her people would take too kindly to that."

Reed had to agree with that assessment. Which left only one thing they could do.

"We'd have to use the transporter," Trip continued, echoing his own thoughts. "That's the only option we have, really."

"What about the interference from that power source?" Archer asked.

"We should be able to compensate."

"And what if the Sarkassians detect it?" Archer asked. "We end up square in the middle of another planet's internal power struggles. And it's just not our business."

Reed got the feeling the captain was talking to himself as much as anyone else.

"We have to ask ourselves, what is our business here?" O'Neil said quietly.

"Good point," Trip said. "As far as I'm concerned, it's real simple. I want to know what the Sarkassians were up to down at that outpost, and if it had anything to do with what happened to Ensign Hart."

"Exactly," Reed said. "I think we have a better chance of getting answers to those questions from Roan than from Ambassador Valay."

"There is another aspect to the situation we must consider," T'Pol said.

Archer nodded. "Go on."

"I believe we can safely infer that the jamming beam was initiated at Ambassador Valay's request."

"That seems obvious enough," Archer said.

"So we must ask ourselves—why?"

Reed thought the answer to that seemed obvious as well. "As Commander Tucker suggested, it may be a civil war. She wanted to prevent Roan from calling in help."

"But the jamming beam is designed to affect all message traffic—outgoing and incoming."

Reed suddenly realized what T'Pol was getting at. "It's not just Roan that Valay wants to stop from talking to the government. It's everyone."

"Yes. And by far the most likely reason for preventing such contact is because it would undermine her position."

"So the commodore was telling the truth," Archer said. "She's acting against the express wishes of her government."

"The possibility must be considered," T'Pol said.

Everyone at the table was silent a moment.

"Actually," she added, "I would consider it a probability."

"Well would you look at this," Trip said. "The worm has turned."

T'Pol turned in his direction, and raised an eyebrow. "I beg your pardon?"

"Figure of speech," Trip said. "Just means that you're not usually the one who argues for getting involved in things like this."

"I am not arguing for any particular course of action at the moment," she replied. "I am merely making an observation."

"One which suggests we should regard Roan as the legitimate representative of the Sarkassian people, and enter the conflict on his side," Archer said.

"I do not favor entering the conflict, sir," T'Pol said. "Not at the present time."

"All due respect, sir," Reed said, "I do believe you're looking at the situation in the wrong way. Saving Roan's life is not a strategic move. It's a humanitarian gesture."

"The road to hell, and all that," Trip said.

Reed shot him an angry glance.

"Another figure of speech, Commander?" T'Pol asked.

Trip nodded. "One of my favorites. Meaning the best intentions sometimes have a way of backfiring on you."

"Backfiring?"

Trip waved a hand at her. "Never mind."

"Something's not right here. I feel it." Archer frowned.

"Sir?" Trip asked.

"Never mind, Commander. All right, everyone. Thank you. Thank you all." Archer looked around the table, weighing his options. Reed could almost see the wheels turning in his head.

"Damn it," he said finally. "I'm going to get a reputation."

Reed smiled. "So we're going to rescue the commodore?"

The captain nodded. "I'd like to. If—T'Pol? Can we rig up a little jamming beam of our own? Something that would prevent the Sarkassians from discovering what we're up to."

"I am not convinced their sensors have the capability to detect a transporter beam under optimum circumstances. Nonetheless, modifying one of our low-energy sensor beams to obtain the desired result should be possible."

"Good. Get on it."

"Wait a second," Trip said. "They can construct

a jamming beam that can automatically detect and smother any transmission on the spectrum, and you don't think they can pick out a matter-transfer beam? Doesn't make much sense to me."

"I based my conclusions on extensive sensor logs. However . . ." T'Pol nodded. "Your point has merit. There are inconsistencies in their technological development."

"People," the captain interrupted. "I'm sure this is an important point, but right now we have a rescue operation to attend to."

"One last thing, sir," Reed said. "Commodore Roan looks like he could be in need of medical assistance."

"Of course. Hoshi, have Dr. Phlox meet us at the transporter." The captain looked around then, and nodded. "All right, everyone. Dismissed. Trip, Malcolm, you're with me."

"Aye, sir," Reed said. As they headed toward the turbolift, he checked the time. By his reckoning, Roan had about five minutes left of breathable air.

Approximately. The word worried him.

Reed had had his molecules successfully scrambled and unscrambled by the transporter before, so he wasn't quite as paranoid as some of the crew about using it. Still, he had to admit he was relieved when the beam in front of him coalesced into the complete, recognizable form of Commodore Roan.

His relief was short-lived, though—he'd been right about the blood. The commodore's robe was soaked with it.

Roan looked around the transporter room in surprise. Disorientation showed in his eyes.

"Matter transmission," the commodore said. His voice was weak. "We are familiar with the theory, but—"

Roan tried to step forward, and wobbled. His legs folded beneath him, and he sat down hard right at the edge of the transporter platform.

Phlox was there instantly, his tricorder out in front of him.

"Extensive burns on the right half of his body— severe dehydration, oxygen deprivation, exhaustion."

"I'm quite all right, Doctor, I assure you." The commodore put his hands on the platform and started to stand. "I must—"

"What you must do is rest, sir," Phlox said forcefully. He gripped Roan's shoulder and kept him from rising. "You are far from all right."

"The blood on his robe?" Archer asked.

"Not mine," Roan said. "My aide's. We were ambushed."

"Ambassador Valay," the captain said.

"Yes. She—" Roan sighed heavily, and shook his head. "I did not expect this from her. Or those she represents. Things are worse than I feared."

"We need to get you to sickbay," Phlox said, shutting the tricorder. "And conduct a thorough examination."

"We don't have time for a thorough examination, Doctor," Roan said. "Ambassador Valay's actions are part of a larger schism within my government. Unless I can move fast to contain the damage, a civil war is imminent."

"Valay's acting on her own," Archer said.

Roan shook his head. "No. I've known her for years. She is not capable of such—"

"She's jamming all frequencies in and out of the system." Archer went on to explain what they'd discovered.

"But this is—" He shook his head. "Totally unlike her. I cannot understand it, Captain."

"There's a lot I don't understand, Commodore. Starting with the purpose of your outpost. The history of the war between you and the Ta'alaat. Among other things."

Roan fell silent.

"Don't you think it's time you told us what was happening here?"

"I am not sure what is happening here," Roan said. At that moment, he looked exhausted, and old, and confused. Seeing that expression on his face, Reed was suddenly catapulted back in time, back to the moment outside Goridian's cell, when Valay emerged, her robe splattered with blood.

There was a connection there—Reed knew it. But for the life of him, he couldn't see what it was.

"Help me up, please," Roan said, extending his hand.

The captain took it, and pulled Roan to his feet. The commodore straightened his robe.

"Someone once said to me that relationships have to be built on trust." The commodore's eyes sought out Reed then, and he smiled. "It is time for me to trust someone, Captain. Let us find someplace to talk, and I will tell you everything."

"Excuse me," Phlox interrupted. "You can begin by telling me what your species likes to eat and drink. You are badly in need of nourishment, sir."

Roan nodded. "I will gladly do that."

"Why don't we use my dining room?" Archer said. "We can talk and get something to eat."

"Let's use this as well, Commodore," Phlox said, wheeling forward the gurney he'd brought with him to the transporter room. "You are still very weak."

Roan shook his head. "No."

"Commodore . . ."

"I can walk, Doctor. Thank you."

They all filed out of the transporter room then, Archer in the lead, Roan a step behind, moving gingerly.

Reed brought up the rear. At the door, he stopped.

There was sand from the outpost on the transporter-room floor. Roan must have had it on his shoes when he'd beamed aboard.

The image resonated in his mind, and he remembered.

Fourteen

"IT'S SILICON, ALL RIGHT," Trip said. "Never seen anything like this before."

They'd been in the tunnel for about five minutes. Reed was still monitoring the captain's party through Ensign Hart's com, but he was starting to get a lot of static. Interference from the power source ahead of them.

"I don't understand," Reed said. "Why silicon? It's not a particularly strong material."

"No, it's not." Trip ran one gloved hand along the tunnel wall, then turned back to his tricorder. "Picking up another layer underneath it, though—a heavier material of some kind. Titanium, looks like. A frame to hang the silicon on."

"So the silicon is functional?" Reed asked. "For . . . ?"

"What do you usually use silicon for? It's a conductor. Energy transmission. Power relays of some kind."

"You don't need power relays this size."

"We don't," Trip said. "Maybe whoever built the tunnels did."

"For what purpose?"

"Right now I couldn't tell you. We'll know a lot more once we reach the power source. Every tunnel starts out from there—like spokes comin' off the hub of a wheel. Tricorder says we're about halfway there."

A loud burst of static came over the com.

"Ensign Hart?"

"Here, sir." He could barely make out her voice.

"What's your situation?"

Static. Then silence. Then more static, and what sounded like the word "separating."

Reed tried to boost his signal, and saw he was already at maximum.

"I say again," he tried, practically shouting, "what is your situation?"

Her reply was inaudible.

"Damn," Reed said.

"Not a surprise. This thing's just about useless, too." Trip snapped the tricorder shut. "Pretty clear where we're going, anyway."

"I'd prefer we knew what was waiting there," Reed said.

"Yeah, well . . ." Trip's voice trailed off. "We don't."

They walked on, Reed still in the lead. He set a faster pace, wishing that he'd been more insistent about beaming down a fuller security complement. Especially once he'd seen how much the power source ahead of them was affecting their tricorders. Whoever had attacked the outpost could be waiting in the central chamber for them. For the captain.

Procedure, Reed thought. *There need to be standard landing party regulations for this kind of situation.*

He knew how that suggestion would go over with the captain. Archer liked being in the thick of things, having the ability to gauge a situation for himself rather than sitting on his hands, tied by regulations. Reed felt just the opposite—to his way of thinking, regulations made quicker decision-making possible, particularly in time-sensitive situations. Regulations eliminated the gray areas. Regulations—

He thought of Alana, in her quarters, the Corbett wet and ruined on the table behind her.

"Malcolm," she'd said. *"It's a stupid regulation."*

In the tunnel, Reed turned to his left and reached for the com. Time to check in on her. And the others, of course.

That motion saved his life.

As he turned, he glimpsed a flicker of light out of the corner of his eye, about waist-high. He'd been walking too fast, preoccupied with his thoughts, or he would have seen it before. He should have seen it before. A pencil-thin beam, stretching across the tunnel.

Rather, it would have been, had he not been standing in its path.

An alarm. A booby trap. And he'd tripped it.

The next few seconds seemed to happen in slow motion.

"Back!" he shouted over the com without turning, because he was still walking forward, and he had to use that momentum, as he yelled he pushed off with his right foot and jumped, and in the lighter gravity of the planetoid felt for a second as if he were flying.

Then the force of the explosion caught him, and he really was flying, windmilling through the air, vaguely aware of the tunnel walls hurtling past him.

He slammed into the ground face-first, and heard something crack.

My helmet. Explosive decompression, he thought, his heart racing, his mind picturing the alien corpses above, expecting to feel the air rushing out of his suit any second.

But nothing happened.

He lay there a moment, stunned, then got to his feet. Something in his neck was twisted—but otherwise he seemed fine. Miraculous.

He turned around and saw that where the tunnel had been, there was now a mountain of rubble.

"Trip!" Reed shouted into the com. "Trip!"

No reply.

Reed switched to another channel. Still nothing. The blast had happened so quickly—Trip would have had to react instantly to get out of the way. Otherwise . . .

"Commander Tucker!" he shouted again. "Are you there? Come in!"

There was nothing on the com. Not even static.

He switched to the channel he'd been monitoring Hart on. Still nothing.

The com could have been damaged in the fall—maybe the cracking he'd heard was the sound of it shattering.

Or there could be no one out there to hear him. Not Trip, not Alana, not anyone on the captain's team. Whoever had set this booby trap might have set another.

He moved back toward the collapsed tunnel, thinking he could dig through it and reach Trip. But once he actually laid his hands on the rubble, he realized instantly that wouldn't work. The top layer consisted of fragments of the duranium framework—and the pieces were far too heavy to move.

But maybe he didn't need to move them.

He took out his phase pistol and fired it at the biggest piece of rubble he could see. After a single sustained burst, the duranium vaporized.

Reed smiled tightly, and targeted another piece of rubble.

Then he saw that single burst had drained the weapons charge by twenty percent.

He sighed, lowered the pistol, and holstered it. Blasting his way through to Trip wouldn't work. So the only way to reach him, then, to find out if he was still alive—was to go forward.

Where—odds were—whoever had set that trap was waiting.

Reed didn't have to walk long before a faint yellow glow appeared ahead of him. Drawing the phase pistol again, he inched along the tunnel wall until he was right next to that light. Then he leaned around the corner. He glimpsed orange-yellow light and, beyond it, the suggestion of open space.

He flattened himself against the wall again and waited. Ten seconds. Twenty. Nothing. No reaction.

He looked again, longer this time. No sign of movement. He stepped out into the center of the tunnel.

The light filled the opening before him, shimmering and throbbing with a life of its own. It obscured whatever lay beyond, like a curtain of opaque material, though he again got the sense of a large open space, with some rough shapes and bright colors visible. Any details, however, eluded him.

Reed reached out with one hand and touched the light.

It pulsed with energy. He felt it through his glove. A forcefield of some kind, he guessed.

Reed pushed on it with his hand—gently at first, then harder.

His arm went through the curtain into the chamber beyond.

He cried out in surprise, and pulled back. He looked his arm over carefully, searching for signs of damage to the suit, and found none. He pushed his arm through the light again, and then pulled it out. He shook it in the air, once, twice. Nothing wrong with the suit. Nothing wrong with him.

He took a deep breath, and stepped forward. For a second, it was like trying to walk under water. He felt resistance. He pushed through it, and into the chamber.

The light inside was much brighter than it had appeared from without. No longer an orange-yellow glow, but a yellowish white—the harsh glare of a spotlight. He blinked once as his eyes adjusted. The chamber came into focus. He took it all in with a single, sweeping glance.

It was circular, perhaps oval, sixty feet around. The floor was the same sandy color as the tunnels had been, the steel gray walls gently sloping upward to a dome perhaps twenty feet above him. Spaced all around the chamber, every half-dozen feet, were openings like the one he'd just come through, filled with the same kind of pulsing curtain of light.

In front of one of those, almost directly across from him, something lay on the ground. He moved closer, and saw it was an environmental suit—one of *Enterprise*'s. Almost instantly, he realized who it belonged to.

Alana.

Why had she taken it off? Had someone taken it off her? Didn't matter. Without the suit, she was dead. Unless . . .

Reed reached down to his side, and found the tricorder still attached to his suit. Thank God the blast hadn't torn it loose. He flipped it open and checked the atmosphere inside the chamber. Four-to-one nitrogen-to-oxygen ratio, a smattering of other inert gases . . .

Breathable.

He took off his helmet, and surveyed the chamber again.

Where was she?

He glanced down at the tricorder. No life signs anywhere within range, but . . .

He was reading a minute variation in air temperature—coming, he realized an instant later, from the ground, where her environmental suit lay.

Body heat, he realized a second later. The chamber was on the cool side—and Alana had left traces of her presence here in the increased temperature readings he was picking up.

If he was quick enough, he could use those to track her.

Seconds later, he'd recalibrated the tricorder. Not much after that, he was standing in front of another of the chamber openings. The readings indicated she'd gone through here.

Putting away the tricorder, he drew his phase pistol and stepped through the curtain of light before him.

This time, it was not so much like walking under water as pushing through a huge snowdrift. The skin on his face tingled, as if warmed by a very bright sun.

He pushed on. Ten seconds, he estimated. Fifteen. Suddenly, the resistance was gone. The light was dimmer, the air thinner, filled with a faint, lingering smell that he couldn't quite place, and Reed looked up and saw he was in one corner of the single largest interior space he'd ever seen in his life.

He tilted his head back and could see no roof. He looked across and could barely make out the opposite wall.

At first he thought it was a cave—a vast chamber carved out of the planetoid itself by natural geologic processes. Then he took in the sharp angles of the walls as they pitched upward to the ceiling and out of sight, the smooth floor, and realized he was wrong.

He was inside the pyramid he'd seen from the shuttle.

It was bigger than he would have guessed—it had to be a quarter mile from the corner he stood in to the one opposite him. And though his first impression had been of a vast, empty space, he saw now that he was wrong, that the chamber was full of freestanding structures, the size of a man, the shape of a book stood on its end. There had to be hundreds of them—maybe even thousands. They reminded him of nothing so much as tombstones.

He took out his tricorder and scanned for life signs again. Still nothing. If Alana was here, she was hidden. Which was quite possible given the fact that the entire pyramid—the floors, the walls, even the tombstone-like structures scattered around the chamber—seemed to be composed of the same alloy he'd detected from space. Or rather, hadn't been able to detect.

More than ever, Reed wanted a sample of it.

He stepped forward, and suddenly became aware of a noise, barely audible, coming from very nearby.

It sounded like someone talking, though he couldn't pick out what was being said, much less identify the voice. Or voices.

He drew his phase pistol again, and stepped forward carefully, in the direction the noise was coming from, trying to be as quiet as possible. As he walked, he became aware again of the odor he had smelled when first entering the pyramid.

And this time, he was able to place it.

It was the smell of electricity—the air crackled

with it. Instinctively he knew he was in the middle of whatever had been causing all the distortion in their sensor readings.

That smell took him back twenty years, back to Earth, the summer after his disastrous second year of school, when his parents had sent him to spend time with his aunt and uncle at their country estate in Sussex. One night, a series of lightning strikes had burned down several cottages on the grounds. Reed remembered standing with his aunt and uncle on a hill overlooking the estate, smelling not just the fire, but the air around him.

"It smells like a pool," he remembered saying to his uncle.

"Like chlorine, Malcolm," the man had said. "You get that smell when electricity passes through oxygen. That's what makes ozone."

Reed had stayed silent then, watching the storm rage, feeling the electricity, the power gathered in the air around him.

He felt the same kind of power here, and wondered what it was all for.

Reed walked on, the noise drawing him toward the center of the pyramid, staying behind the tombstone-like structures as much as possible, well aware that he could be heading right toward whoever had set that the booby trap for him.

The farther in he went toward the center, the easier that got to do. The rectangles became more concentrated—it was like walking through a graveyard, dodging from tombstone to tombstone, trying to remain unseen.

Then he stepped out from behind one of the larger stones and saw Alana.

For a second he was paralyzed, unable to move.

Reed had been in deep space for over a year. He'd seen a lot in that time—death, and some things he thought worse than death: the captain and Trip half-absorbed by an alien creature. The Suliban rebels blown to pieces by the Cabal. Even before *Enterprise*, he'd been witness to some fairly gruesome sights. As a cadet, he was touring the Cochrane Research Facility on Sirius IV when the reactor blew. Twenty people were trapped in the radioactive core—he stood in the shielded observation room and watched them die. One of those twenty had been a fellow cadet—a first-year named John Mayhill, an English boy whom Reed had never really gotten to know.

Mayhill's last few hours he spent standing opposite Reed, the two of them staring at each other and talking over a comlink from opposite sides of the window. The weaker Mayhill got, the braver he seemed to become, the more stoic. Try hard as he could, Reed had been just the opposite. He couldn't keep the tears from flowing when the boy was no longer strong enough to stand.

Once in a while, Reed still had nightmares about that day.

But even that hadn't affected him the way looking at Alana did right now.

She lay on the ground directly in front of the rectangular shapes—only to use the word *lay* was wrong, because she wasn't just lying there, she was twitching, her arms and legs flailing everywhere, and he would have called it a seizure, except he'd never seen a seizure like this before.

She was in agony.

The words coming out of her mouth were gibberish.

Sickbay, Reed thought, and even though he knew it was useless, he dropped his phase pistol on the ground and flipped open his communicator.

Nothing but static.

He dropped down next to Alana, and took her shoulders. She shook uncontrollably, randomly, like a drop of water splattering its way across a hot griddle. As if a thousand volts of electricity were shooting through her.

"Easy," Reed said. "I'm here. It's all right. I'm here."

His words had no effect.

He had to get her back to *Enterprise*. Now. Which meant carrying her back to the chamber where her suit was, and back through the tunnels to the shuttlecraft.

He couldn't do that while she was seizing like this.

For a second, he thought about stunning her with the phase pistol. He glanced around, looking to see where he'd dropped it.

His eyes fell on a man lying on the ground ten feet away. He'd been hidden from Reed's view by one of the stones. No, not a man. An alien. His skin pale, almost translucent. His eyes were open wide as well.

Wide, and unseeing. He looked dead. Who was he? Did he have something to do with what had happened to Alana?

On the ground next to him, Reed's tricorder started beeping. Life signs approaching.

He heard voices behind him, and turned to see Captain Archer, heading toward them at a run.

Fifteen

"THREE WORLD WARS," Archer said. "The last one almost destroyed our planet. It took us a hundred years to rebuild civilization—and reach the stars again."

"In such a short span of time—those achievements are remarkable. I congratulate you," Roan said.

"Human beings have a hunger for achievement," Phlox said. "One of the many reasons I took on this assignment—to be a part of their successes."

"And your race again, Doctor—Denobulans, you said?"

Phlox nodded. "Yes. We are relative newcomers to space as well—at least compared to the Vulcans."

He smiled at T'Pol, who sat across the table

from him. There were six of them crowded into the captain's mess—Archer and Trip at the two heads of the table, Roan and Phlox on one side, Reed and T'Pol on the other. Most of the conversation had consisted of the captain talking about Starfleet, and its development, pushing others to get involved at times, letting the commodore focus on eating and getting his strength back.

"We are all newcomers compared to the Vulcans," Roan said.

T'Pol studied him curiously. "You are familiar with our history, then? Our race?"

"We are."

"Surprising. In studying our database, I find no record of any encounters with the Sarkassians."

"Oh, we have never met Vulcans. I did not mean to imply otherwise. All I meant to say is that we have knowledge of your people."

"How?"

"Through our records, of course," Roan said, suddenly looking slightly uncomfortable.

T'Pol looked to press the question—but the captain spoke first.

"How's your food, Commodore?"

"Excellent. This—" He pointed with his fork to the plate before him.

"Eggs," Archer supplied. "An omelette."

"A frittata actually, Captain," Phlox said.

"Wonderful," Roan said. "Very substantive."

"I believe there's more," Archer put in.

"No, no—I am quite full." Roan pushed his plate away. "Thank you. You were right about the food on your ship, Lieutenant Reed. Another remarkable achievement. My years of service would have passed much more pleasurably were our cooks able to achieve similar results."

"We'll see if we can get you some recipes," Archer said.

"You have made some remarkable technological achievements yourself," T'Pol said. "The jamming beam Ambassador Valay employed, for example. The level of computing power required to detect and almost instantaneously counter transmissions all across the EM frequency is staggering."

Roan nodded. "Yes, it is a staggering achievement."

Yet to Reed's eyes, he seemed uncomfortable talking about it. The captain noticed too.

"Forgive my saying so, Commodore," Archer said, "but you don't sound especially proud of it."

"No. I am not." Roan sighed. "You know, I have been sitting here this entire time, trying to enjoy this excellent meal and yet knowing that it comes at a price—the price of trusting you with a secret my people have kept for hundreds of years."

"Hold on a minute," the captain said. "There's no price on our assistance, Commodore. That's not why we agreed to help you."

"Not at all. No price on the treatment we give

you," Phlox added. Reed noticed that the doctor had slipped out his tricorder again and was scanning the commodore. "Speaking of which, we need to attend to those burns you suffered, sir. They must be quite painful."

Roan waved him away. "I am used to pain. Especially when it comes to burns—as you can see." He pointed at the mottled patch of red and brown skin that ran down the side of his face.

"I can give you something to make you more comfortable," Phlox said.

"No. I need my faculties about me, Doctor. Both to deal with Valay, and to explain the situation to you."

Roan was silent a moment. Everyone waited for him to continue.

"We were discussing technology. Your jamming beam," Archer prompted.

"No." Roan shook his head. "Not ours."

"Ambassador Valay's jamming beam. Excuse me."

"No," Roan said again. "You miss my point. The jamming beam—the technology as a whole—none of it is ours."

"Wait a second." Trip asked, "Not yours? So whose is it?"

Reed had a sudden, sneaking suspicion that he knew. "The Ta'alaat. That's why your people are at war."

"No, no." Roan managed a small smile. "And

yet—in a way, you are right. Technology is why we're fighting. Technology, and my people's appropriation of it."

"I'm a little confused, Commodore," Archer said. "If it's not the Ta'alaat's technology, then why are they so upset?"

"Because they feel their claim to it is greater. Though most of the Ta'alaat would prefer that no one have access to the technology—except, of course, for its rightful owners."

"Who are—" the captain prompted.

"We do not know exactly. No one does."

"Now you lost me," Trip said.

"It's quite simple. For the past several hundred years, my people have progressed, and prospered, not so much by reaping the fruits of our own efforts, but by searching out and uncovering machines left behind by another race. Machines that—even in their decaying condition—contain scientific advancements far beyond what we are currently capable of. The technology involved—it often seems miraculous."

Things suddenly clicked into place for Reed.

"They built the outpost on the planetoid below—this race you're talking about," he said.

"That's right. Built it, and at some point approximately ten thousand years ago, abandoned it wholesale."

Reed remembered too the series of shallow depressions he'd seen on the planetoid's surface then, and realized what they were. Excavation pits. "You were conducting a dig down there. An archaeological dig."

"Yes. Our scientists had just broken through to the tunnel complex when the attack occurred."

"Commodore," Phlox said. "I wonder if you have records detailing the sorts of machines your scientists discovered. That information could be of assistance to us—in determining what happened to our crewman."

"It is more than likely," Roan said. "Unfortunately, those records are down on the planet's surface—and we are here."

"So who were these people who built the outpost?" Archer asked.

"We don't know. Over the centuries, we've discovered records throughout this sector calling them by various names. The Anu'anshee, the Krytallans, the Irakua. We have never been able to decipher their language to determine what they called themselves."

"The Anu'anshee," T'Pol broke in. "Interesting. If memory serves, a race by that name appears within the Vulcan database as one of the earliest known warp-capable species in the galaxy."

"That is not surprising. Our scientists deduced that thousands of years ago, they established a substantial presence throughout the quadrant."

"This still doesn't explain why the Ta'alaat and

you are at war," Trip said. "Why do they care about this technology so much?"

"Because to them, the Anu'anshee are gods—their gods." Roan took another sip of water. "We first encountered the Ta'alaat several hundred years ago, during one of our planet's earliest warp flights. They were a far more primitive race than we, having just made the transition from a nomadic to an agricultural civilization. We had intended to leave their planet without making contact—until we picked up some anomalous power signatures from within their cities."

"Power sources—like the one in the pyramid here," Reed said.

"That's right," Roan said. "We found a field generator there of such advanced design and complexity that it was judged necessary to examine it further. The generator, unfortunately, was housed within one of their temples. A holy place."

"I'm beginning to get a sense of what's involved here," Archer asked.

"Me too. So you booted them out of their temple?" Trip asked. "Yeah, I can see how that might cause some tension."

"I'm not trying to condone or apologize for what happened hundreds of years ago," Roan said. "Only to explain. Our people were prepared for an initial outburst of hatred—we had already decided to share the fruits of the technology with the Ta'alaat, as a way to make up for our trespass.

But we underestimated how deeply they venerated these sites."

"If you want to see somebody's blood boil, start disrespecting their religion," Trip said.

"If by boiling blood you mean to say they were angry . . . well, that is an understatement, Commander. We had no idea the lengths to which they would go on behalf of their beliefs. Within a hundred years, the Ta'alaat had made the jump from throwing stones to using phased-energy weapons against us—and with the passing of time, their attacks only get deadlier. This horror on the planet below is the worst yet. Sixty people dead—sixty innocent scientists."

"Forgive me, sir," T'Pol said, "but you must be aware that from the perspective of the Ta'alaat, they are as guilty as any who profane their temple."

"In war, there is a difference between targeting soldiers—and killing scientists."

"Logically speaking, it is all a matter of perspective."

"This explains why Goridian and the Ta'alaat hate your people," Captain Archer said. "It doesn't explain the fight between you and Ambassador Valay."

"It's all part of the same fight, Captain," Roan said. "There are those of us—myself included—who think the only way out of this situation is a reversal of the last several centuries of policy. Then there are others—such as Ambassador

Valay—who want to consider what's happening between the Ta'alaat and my people a war, and respond accordingly."

"From what you're telling us, that would be a one-sided war," Reed said.

"The Ta'alaat have weapons of their own at this point," Roan said, "But the fight would be short. No—*fight* is the wrong term. It would be a massacre."

"And again—that explains why Valay killed Goridian. It doesn't explain why she attacked you."

"My reputation," Roan said. "Who I am. You see, in the past, my position on the Ta'alaat was much more in line with Ambassador Valay's. I was something of a hero, I am forced to say. Because of certain events."

"Dar Shalaan," Reed guessed, and from the look of surprise that crossed the commodore's face, he knew he was right. "But what does killing you get her?"

"I have been trying to figure that out," Roan said. "I can only assume that she hopes to pin my death on the Ta'alaat, and thereby win support for her cause."

"History shows us that such extreme actions rarely achieve their desired ends," T'Pol said. "Your death could have exactly the opposite result—it could win sympathy for your cause."

"The only thing your death does for certain is

increase the enmity between your position and hers," the captain said.

"I don't know how much more bitter the struggle could get," Roan said. "In my opinion, we have been on the verge of civil war for several months now. No one wins if that scenario comes to pass."

"That's not exactly true," Reed said. "Strategically speaking, the Ta'alaat win in that instance."

"Your point being that the ambassador is a Ta'alaat spy? I hardly think so," Roan said. "She did, after all, kill Goridian. No, there is simply no way of determining her plan at the moment. What I need to do now is to contact my government."

T'Pol and Archer exchanged looks.

But before either of them could speak, Phlox stood up. "I'm afraid that in fact what you must do now, Commodore, is come with me to sickbay. Where I can finish examining you, and insure that the injuries you suffered previously have not worsened."

Roan shook his head. "I appreciate your concern, Doctor, but the situation here is simply too urgent to allow—"

"I recognize that tone in Phlox's voice, Commodore," Captain Archer said. "Better do what he says, or he may sedate you right here and now and do the examination on the mess table."

Archer smiled as he spoke, but there was an undercurrent of command in his voice. The captain wanted Roan to leave with Phlox so that he could discuss the situation with his senior officers.

"Well." Roan looked from the captain to the doctor, and nodded slowly. Reed had the feeling the commodore knew exactly what was going on. "We wouldn't want that to happen, would we?"

"No," Archer said. "We wouldn't."

"All right," Roan said. "Sickbay it is, then."

"Good. Follow me then. Captain, I will inform you of the commodore's condition as soon as possible. Good morning, everyone."

He left the room. Roan followed, but stopped in the open doorway, and turned back to Archer.

"Whatever you decide to do, Captain—you've saved my life. I appreciate that. Thank you."

"You're welcome," Archer said.

Roan stepped through the door, and it slid shut.

"What a mess," Trip said. "Not only have we landed ourselves smack in the middle of a war, it's a civil war, to boot."

"We must use the transporter to send the commodore back to the planetoid's surface, and withdraw," T'Pol said.

"I'm with her, sir," Trip said. "We saved his life, and that's a good thing, but now it's time for us to leave."

"Before we find out what happened to Ensign Hart?" Reed asked.

"We know what happened to Ensign Hart,"

T'Pol said. "She is dead. If you are suggesting that we return to the planet's surface to search for clues as to what caused the behavior that ultimately led to her death, I believe that to be a foolish course of action. The information we might find is not worth the risk of involving ourselves in this war."

Trip sighed heavily. "I have to agree with her, Malcolm. I'm sorry. Even forgetting about Hart for a second, we go down to that outpost again we're just asking to get shot at."

"I'm not so sure," Archer said quietly.

"Captain?" Trip looked at him with surprise. "You can't be thinking of getting involved here. It'll be the Suliban refugees all over again—people'll get wind of this, the same way Zobral did, and they'll be banging down our door for food and weapons and God knows what else."

"I don't think so," Archer said. "What Valay is doing—killing Goridian, antagonizing us, going after the commodore—my gut tells me it's outside the context of this political battle with Roan."

T'Pol looked at him quizzically. "Your gut?"

"It's a human expression. My instincts."

"I must disagree with you then, sir. Instincts are not a reliable basis for decision. Vulcans trust precedent. Probability."

"Trust me then." Archer smiled. "Because precedent shows, that in all probability—I'm right about this."

Archer smiled. T'Pol's expression didn't change. Trip threw up his hands in disgust.

"Oh for Pete's sake. I don't know what the heck we have these meetings for anyway. No changin' your mind once it's made up."

"What course of action do you propose, Captain?" T'Pol asked.

"I'm thinking about that," Archer said, walking to the window. He looked out at the planetoid below.

Reed followed his gaze, down past the Sarkassian ships, to the outpost itself.

His gut—his instincts, the little voice inside his head, whatever you wanted to call it—told him the answers were all down there. To everything. Goridian's actions. Valay's responses. And most especially . . .

What had happened to Alana.

Sixteen

"HOLD HER STEADY," Phlox said. The doctor had an ampule in one hand, and was drawing its contents into the hypodermic he held in his other.

Alana lay on the gurney in front of him. Reed stood on one side of it, Trip the other. Each had hold of one of Alana's arms. Bishop had her ankles. Keeping her still wasn't easy. The seizures hadn't subsided at all, were if anything more intense now than they'd been when Reed had first found her. He wondered how long this could go on for.

He wondered how much more her body could take.

"What the hell is the matter with her?" Trip asked, grimacing as he tried to keep hold of her wrist. Sweat had broken out on his brow; he seemed rattled by what was happening in a way

Reed had never seen him rattled before. Hell, they were all rattled—Trip, the captain, himself, even Phlox.

The entire landing party—as well as Phlox and Ensign Cutler—was gathered on the shuttle deck. The landing party plus one, actually—that one being the alien Reed had discovered lying next to Hart inside the pyramid, who had turned out to be comatose, not dead. Cutler stood over him now, tricorder in hand, taking readings.

"If I knew what was the matter with Ensign Hart, Commander, I would fix it," Phlox said irritably.

"No clues at all as to what's causing this?" Archer asked.

"No. In layman's terms, her brain is short-circuiting, and I cannot find the fault in the wiring. She has no history of such episodes. And I find no evidence of physical trauma." He studied the hypo a moment, checking the dosage. "There."

Phlox brought the hypo down and in one swift motion jabbed it into Alana's shoulder—the one Reed was holding. Reed winced sympathetically.

Alana didn't notice at all.

"That should help," Phlox said. "Give it a few minutes."

"What did you give her?" Archer asked.

"Diaphragen," Phlox said.

"Isn't that poison?" Reed asked.

"In this instance, it acts as a paralyzing agent,"

said Phlox. "I cannot stop the seizures—but I can help stop their physiological expression."

"Why not just sedate her? Put her to sleep?"

"No. The diaphragen paralyzes only the large muscle groups. Putting her completely under while she's seizing so violently could have an affect on her autonomic systems as well—her breathing. I don't want to risk it. Perhaps in sickbay, but not here."

Alana twitched right then, almost tearing loose from Reed's grasp. Like she'd been shot through with a hundred thousand volts. Short-circuited, just like the doctor had said.

Electricity.

The smell in the pyramid—the air, crackling with energy.

He and Trip held Alana down till the worst of it passed. Then he told Phlox what he remembered.

"Interesting," the doctor said. "A powerful enough electric shock—that is consistent with some of these readings, at least. But you saw no weapon."

"Or machinery of any recognizable kind," Reed said.

"We need to get back down there then," Phlox said. "See if we can discover what caused this."

"Start by looking at my tricorder readings, Doctor," Archer said. "We haven't had a chance to examine them at all."

The captain, Hoshi, and Bishop had been there

as well—they were the ones whose life signs Reed had picked up as he sat in the pyramid, cradling Hart in his arms. They'd separated from Alana when the tunnel they were in had branched off in different directions. Though Reed only found that out later, of course, after they'd gotten Alana—and the alien—back to the shuttlecraft. Trip was waiting there too. The reunion was a little less joyful than it would ordinarily have been, however, given Hart's condition.

Which suddenly seemed to be improving.

"Doctor," Reed said, drawing Phlox's attention.

"Ah. The diaphragen seems to be taking effect. Good."

Reed let go of Alana's arm. It flopped on the gurney, then lay still.

"I need to get her to sickbay. Right away." Phlox began securing the restraints on the gurney. Reed helped him.

"What about him?" Archer asked, nodding over his shoulder to the alien.

"He doesn't show any of the same symptoms, if that's what you're asking," Phlox said. "I haven't had time to study his readings in depth, but from what I can tell—"

The com sounded.

"Bridge to Captain Archer. Bridge to the captain."

That was Mayweather. There was an urgent tone to his voice.

"Archer here."

"Picking up two ships closing fast on our position."

"On my way." Archer turned to Phlox. "Keep me posted on her condition. Everyone else, to your stations."

Trip, Hoshi, and T'Pol followed the captain out the door.

Reed hesitated.

"There's nothing you can do, Lieutenant."

He turned and saw Phlox staring at him.

"Go," the doctor said. "I'll call you the second I know something."

Reed nodded. "All right."

He jogged after Archer and the others.

Emerging from the turbolift, Reed saw that the main viewscreen was filled with the image of a man—humanoid, at any rate—sitting in what looked to be the equivalent of their bridge. He looked to be of the same race as the alien they'd found at the outpost—the same pale, almost translucent skin and snow white hair—although the man on the viewscreen, and for that matter, all the others on the ship that Reed could see, were elongated versions of the survivor they'd found, tall and thin, to the point of what in humans would have been emaciated.

Reed was no expert on body language, but it seemed to him that although the man was speaking in a calm, even tone, and sat still and composed in his chair, he was holding his true feelings in check. And one of those true feelings was definitely anger.

"He doesn't look happy," Reed said out loud.

"It might be it's his outpost down there." Archer assumed his chair. "Kill that audio until we have the translator up."

"Aye, sir." Ensign Carstairs, at Hoshi's station, punched a switch on the console in front of him, and the alien's voice fell silent.

Reed's station had been offline. He brought up a tactical display, and started scanning the two ships for weapons. As he worked, he caught snippets of the conversations taking place around him, from Mayweather—

"—arriving from heading zero-zero-six-mark-four. They hailed us immediately, we responded with standard friendship greetings, and a burst transmission of . . ."

—and Hoshi—

". . . frequency analysis reveals usage is consistent. I'm running the transmission through the Donaldson matrix. That should give us something to start . . ."

—and T'Pol.

"—two ships, combined tonnage roughly equivalent to half of our mass," T'Pol said. "Warp capability."

"Malcolm?"

He looked up to see the captain in his chair, turned to face Reed's station.

"What can you tell me?"

"Let me show you, sir—on the viewscreen."

"All right."

"Travis," Reed said, "can you switch to an exterior view of the ships?"

"Aye, sir," Mayweather said, and a second later, the image of the man who had been talking disappeared from the main screen, and was replaced by a shot of space outside the *Enterprise*.

One of the alien ships occupied a significant portion of the screen.

It looked dangerous—a ship built for warfare. Shaped like nothing so much as an arrowhead, to the naked eye it looked to be made of a single piece of metal, silvery black in color, that would barely have been visible save for a light green glow that outlined it against the blackness of space.

"Nasty," Travis said.

"Designed to look that way." Reed scanned his display, then began reading off the pertinent information.

"Sensors say it has six weapons ports, spaced equidistantly around the hull. Consistent with similar designs for pulsed energy beams. No indication of fusion weapons. The light green glow you see is the shielding—which I think we could punch through with our cannons."

"Let's hope it doesn't come to that," Archer said. "Where's the other ship?"

"Moving to position one hundred eighty degrees apart," T'Pol replied from her station. "Matching orbit."

"Right behind us," Archer said.

"That's optimum attack position. I'd recommend polarizing the hull plating, sir," Reed said.

"Not just yet, Malcolm. Let's try talking."

"Captain." That was Hoshi. Archer swiveled in his chair to face her.

"We've got the translation. We're dealing with an alien race called the Sarkassians, and their commander, a Commodore Roan."

"Good work. Put him back on."

The alien commander's image filled the viewscreen—and at the exact same instant, his voice sounded again. This time, in English.

". . . explain your presence here. We are—"

"Excuse me," the captain said.

The alien commander—Roan—looked up. Surprise crossed his face for an instant, then was replaced by a small smile.

"Your translators are faster than ours," he said.

Archer returned his smile. "We had more to work with. I'm Captain Jonathan Archer, of the *Starship Enterprise*."

"Commodore Roan S'acree, of the *Defender Talbot*. Representing the Sarkassian Empire. You are in our territory, *Enterprise*." The smile was still on

Roan's face, but it wasn't matched by the expression in his eyes.

He was suspicious of them, Reed saw. Very much so.

"I'm sorry." Archer said. "We did not mean to trespass. We were responding to what we thought was a distress signal from the outpost below."

"The outpost has been destroyed," Roan said. "What do you know about that?"

"I can tell you what we saw."

"You trespassed?" Roan's eyes went wide. He no longer tried to hide his anger.

"I told you, we were answering a distress signal." Archer briefly summarized what they'd seen at the outpost, then told him about the survivor they'd found, whom they'd brought back to the *Enterprise*.

"You will transport this man to us immediately."

"He's comatose—my chief medical officer is treating him right now."

"Our medical staff is far more experienced than yours, Captain. Please let us take care of our own."

Archer hesitated. "I'll have our doctor transmit his findings to your staff. They can consult."

"Very well."

Archer nodded to one of the ensigns on duty, who walked hurriedly toward the nearest com.

"I'd also like to invite you and some of your crew to come aboard *Enterprise*," the captain said. "As I think you'll be able to tell from the transmission we sent you, Starfleet is an organization built on the firm foundation of respect for its neighbors—and dedicated to the principles of peace."

"In addition to your principles, you have phased energy weapons and fusion torpedoes," Roan said. "Either of which could have caused the damage to our outpost below."

"We didn't attack your outpost."

Roan nodded. "We shall see."

One of the other Sarkassians suddenly moved into the picture, and whispered something into Roan's ear. His face remained impassive as he listened.

"Captain, I must break off our transmission at this time," Roan said. "I will contact you again in a moment."

The screen went dark.

"They are receiving a signal over subspace frequencies," Hoshi said. "Coded, but I'm sure we could—"

"No," Archer responded quickly. "Not our concern."

They waited. Reed thought to take the opportunity to check up on Alana. But as he reached for the com at his station, he stopped himself.

Phlox said he would contact him when he knew something. Or if her condition changed. So Alana was fine.

But he couldn't shake the image of her lying on the gurney from his mind.

"The *Talbot* is hailing us again, sir."

"Put them through."

Roan's face appeared onscreen.

"Captain Archer," Roan said without preamble. "I have been instructed to read you the following statement. *Enterprise*, your presence in Sarkassian territory is an act of aggression, which we take as indication that hostilities exist between our two peoples. Should you wish to provide an explanation for your presence, it must be given according to the protocols of Contact between the Empire and outside races. Only ministerial-level officials may preside over such contact. Do you wish to provide such an explanation?"

"I've already told you—"

"Captain, do you wish to provide such an explanation to the appropriate government official?"

Reed saw the captain visibly holding his temper. At that second, his display beeped, and he looked down and saw something else.

The two Sarkassian ships had charged their weapons systems.

He raised his head, about to speak, and caught T'Pol's eye. She held up a finger.

Wait.

Archer took a deep breath. "I do wish to provide such an explanation. To the appropriate government official."

Roan gave a curt nod of acknowledgment.

The two ships powered down their weapons.

"Then you are to maintain your present position and await the arrival of an official government delegation."

"About how long until this ambassadorial delegation arrives?" Archer asked.

"Approximately one and a half rotations of the planetoid below us."

"About twenty-six hours, sir," T'Pol added.

"All right," Archer said. "In the meantime . . . in addition to the survivor we found, I have a crewman who was injured while searching the outpost. We're puzzled over what might have caused—"

"I'm sorry, Captain. According to the protocols of Contact, I cannot speak with you further."

"We can go off the record, Commodore."

"I cannot go off the record. I'm sorry."

The screen went dark.

"Seems like this Commodore Roan is on a short leash," Reed said.

Archer turned to T'Pol. "Do we know anything about the Sarkassian Empire? What kind of government they have, where their homeworld is—"

"To the best of my recollection, no. I will, however, conduct a thorough search of the Vulcan database," T'Pol said.

The com at his station sounded.

"Sickbay to Captain Archer."

That was Phlox. Reed forced himself to stay calm.

"Archer here. Go ahead, Doctor."

"There's been a change in Ensign Hart's condition," Phlox said.

"How is she?" Reed blurted out. Something was wrong—he could hear it in the doctor's voice.

"I think," Phlox said hesitantly, "you should come down here."

Seventeen

ENTERPRISE
1/17/2151 0949 HOURS

REED STOPPED AT THE ENTRANCE to sickbay, momentarily confused.

Why was he here? Phlox had summoned him from the bridge. To see what had happened to Alana. Except . . .

He frowned. *No. That was wrong.* Because Alana was dead. And Phlox calling him to sickbay was all in the past, had already happened, days ago, when they'd first returned from the outpost's surface.

He shook his head. This sort of thing had been happening to him all day—memories being triggered randomly, his being forced to relive the painful events of the last few days all over again. Lack of sleep, he supposed, though it had never affected him in quite this way. All he could do was stay focused. And speaking of focused . . .

He remembered why he was here now—to pick up Commodore Roan.

Reed took a deep breath, straightened his shoulders, and walked into sickbay.

"Your timing is perfect, Lieutenant," Phlox said. "We're just finishing up here."

"Everything's all right?" Reed asked.

"Everything is fine," Roan said, pushing himself off the diagnostic bed.

"Not exactly fine," Phlox said. "The commodore's burns are quite extensive. I have given him a numbing agent for the pain. He should return here within the next three hours for another dosage."

"Not necessary," Roan said. "Thank you."

"Lieutenant," Phlox said, clasping his hands behind his back and smiling what Trip referred to as his annoyingly cheerful smile. "Please convey my medical recommendations to the captain."

"I will," Reed said. "But the commodore may not be here in three hours."

Phlox frowned. Roan smiled.

"Your captain's decided to help," the commodore said.

"To help," Reed said. "And to ask for help in return."

Reed had orders to take Roan to the science lab on E-deck. On the way, he told the commodore Archer's plan.

"It seems to me I get the better of this bargain, Lieutenant."

"We value different things, Commodore."

"When will we do this?" Roan asked.

"As soon as T'Pol gives the word. If, of course, you're up to it."

"My burns?" Roan shook his head. "As I said—I am accustomed to such injuries. I'll be fine."

Reed's gaze went to the mottled patch of skin on his neck and face.

"These were much more severe," Roan said, seeing where Reed was looking. "Extensive grafts were required."

"It must have been very painful."

"At that moment—I honestly didn't notice. Later, during recovery—I was in a great deal of pain, yes."

"Not to be overly forward, sir, but—Phlox could do something about the discoloration there."

"As could our doctors. I prefer to leave the burns as they are. They're a reminder."

"Of Dar Shalaan?"

Roan nodded. "Yes." His eyes glazed over then, and Reed could tell he was seeing something other than the corridor they were walking down. "Please, Lieutenant—it is something I prefer not to speak about."

"I'm sorry, sir. I didn't mean to press."

But twenty feet down the corridor, Roan suddenly started talking again.

"Imagine the most important religious shrine on your world. Imagine a city grown up around it over thousands of years, a city devoted to and dependent on it. That was Dar Shalaan—not the Ta'alaat capital, not their largest city, not their economic center, but their most important city, nonetheless. Until I destroyed it."

The words spilled out in a rush, as if the commodore had kept them bottled up for so long they were desperate for escape.

"It was war," Reed offered. "Terrible things happen in war."

"Yes." Roan stopped walking. "It was war. A tactical counterstrike. An accident that no one could have foreseen. A massacre—it was all of those, and one other. My fault. My responsibility."

"When we were talking about Earth history earlier," Reed said, "the captain mentioned our three world wars? Things happened in each of those wars that seemed at the time too horrific for the combatants to ever forget, or forgive. Yet here we are—Starfleet. Representing one world, one people—the past put behind us."

"You *are* one people," Roan said. "That is the point. The Ta'alaat and we are different species."

"But the situation is the same. Our wars were over common resources—things we never dreamed of sharing. The way your war is over the sites the Anu'anshee left behind."

"We tried sharing with the Ta'alaat, Lieutenant. Dar Shalaan was the result."

Roan turned and began walking again.

This time, he really had said his piece on the topic.

He didn't speak again until they reached the lab.

"This is Ensign Hoshi," Reed said. "Our linguistics expert. Hoshi, Commodore Roan."

"Ensign," Roan said. "Pleased to meet you."

"Likewise."

Hoshi sat at one end of a long stainless-steel table, in front of a portable workstation. A handful of the fragments she'd brought back from the outpost lay stacked in a pile next to it. Other fragments were scattered haphazardly across the table.

"Any luck with the translation?" Reed asked.

Hoshi shook her head. "I don't have enough here to work with. There are only fourteen symbols, and I have no way of knowing what they're supposed to represent. They could be hieroglyphs, letters from an alphabet, musical notes. . . ."

"This translation is what your captain wanted my help with?" Roan asked.

"That's right."

Roan picked up one of the fragments and studied it a moment.

"These are *phondrikaar.*"

"Excuse me," Hoshi said. "What was that word?"

"*Phondrikaar.*"

"And what does it mean?"

"It's our name for the alloy these fragments are composed of." He looked over at Reed. "These came from the outpost."

"That's right," the lieutenant said.

"A handful of our Striker-ships utilize this material to avoid sensor detection. They have proven quite effective in battle."

"I don't doubt it," Reed said.

Roan was silent a long moment before replying. "I must admit to mixed emotions here, Lieutenant. Seeing you in possession of a critical piece of our technology . . . it reminds me that although we are allies at the moment, our interests are not necessarily identical."

"And may I remind you of your own words, sir—it's not your technology."

Roan forced a smile. "A fair point. And yet—"

"If it makes a difference—I've been instructed to tell you that we'll return the fragments to you on leaving the system. We're less concerned with them than the information they may contain."

"Well—in any case, I cannot help you. I don't suspect even our experts on the Anu'anshee could. From what I know of our research, Ensign Hoshi, it runs parallel to yours. We've found only a limited number of symbols in this alphabet—if it is an alphabet. And no matter where we find them, they are always arranged in the same pattern. I'm sorry."

Hoshi nodded. "Thank you anyway, sir."

Reed clapped a hand on her shoulder. "Carry on, Ensign."

Hoshi smiled wryly. "Which I gather means keep working at it?"

"I have no orders to the contrary."

"All right." Hoshi shrugged, and turned back to her station.

"Was there anything else, Lieutenant?" Roan asked.

"Yes. One other thing—a quick look through the Vulcan database with me." Reed led him to the other side of the lab, and brought the computer station there online.

"To what purpose?" Roan came and stood by his shoulder.

"The Anu'anshee. We thought that perhaps looking through the records we might find something that could help us determine the purpose of the outpost here. And what sort of machinery might be down there."

"I see. You're still trying to determine what happened to your ensign."

"Yes, sir."

"A remarkable amount of effort for a single member of your crew."

"Some might say we've gone to a remarkable effort on your behalf, Commodore."

Roan laughed. It was the first time Reed had heard him do that.

"Fair enough, Lieutenant. Let us see what the Vulcans know."

The short answer to that was a lot. T'Pol's memory was correct—there were mentions of the Anu'anshee throughout the database. Hundreds of mentions. Most of them they were able to scan and dismiss quickly as irrelevant, apocryphal, inaccurate—fragments of history handed down through the ages as religious texts, or mythology. References to the Anu'anshee as gods with fantastic powers, such as the ability to speak in many tongues at once, to travel great distances in an instant, to bring down mountains, change the course of planets, and so forth. All incredible feats, to be sure, but most of which Reed could have pulled off with the technology at hand on *Enterprise*.

Some of the claims, though, were a bit more fantastic.

" 'Even death would not defeat them, for they moved beyond the substance of this world at will, from one flesh to the next, their essence eternal and unchanging, a part and not a part of this world.' " Reed frowned. "I'm not sure I know what that means."

"I'm sure I don't."

He looked up and saw Hoshi standing next to Roan.

"Sorry," she said. "I couldn't help overhearing."

"It's all right." Reed stood. "Here. Why don't

you handle the database? You've had more experience dealing with it."

Hoshi took his seat, and moved the chair closer to the table. She frowned at the screen.

"Let me start by narrowing the query parameters."

"We don't want to miss anything, Ensign."

"No, trust me Lieutenant. Things like this"—she nodded at the screen—"we want to miss. 'They spoke as our leaders, with the voice of our leaders, in the flesh of our leaders, yet they were gods still.'" She shook her head. "Give me a minute."

Her fingers flew over the keypad. The screen cleared for an instant—then suddenly filled with text again.

Reed smiled. "This is more like it," he said, leaning over her shoulder.

He was looking at a list of perhaps three dozen articles now. Longer entries—more recent ones, with more detailed references to the Anu'anshee. An article reviewing recent Vulcan archaeological digs in the Kandoge and Camus systems—another discussing the etymology of the name Anu'anshee (from the Cyrean word for *collector*, though Hoshi insisted the correct translation of the word was "those who preserve")—and at last, photos of other outposts the Anu'anshee had abandoned. More of the same oddly shaped buildings Reed had seen on the planetoid below.

Hoshi set the images of the outposts to scroll by on the monitor, one at a time.

"Commodore?" Reed asked. "Anything look familiar?"

"It all looks familiar—the Anu'anshee had a very distinctive architectural style. But nothing exactly resembles . . ."

His voice trailed off.

Reed looked down at the screen just in time to see a picture of what looked like the ruins of a city flash by.

"Hold it," he said, putting a hand on Hoshi's shoulder. "Commodore? Did you see something? Recognize something?"

Roan was still staring at the monitor.

"Back up to the last picture, would you, Hoshi?" Reed asked.

The ruined city filled the monitor screen again. The devastation was terrible. Shell of building after building, blackened and broken beyond repair, jagged fingers of metal reaching up to the sky as if in supplication.

Only something was wrong with the image.

In the very middle of the picture, there was a splotch of silver and green.

"Hoshi," he said, pointing.

"I see it," she said, and zoomed in on the image.

The silver and green resolved into a handful of small buildings, untouched by the devastation around them, surrounding a cluster of trees.

"That's not right," Reed said.

Hoshi zoomed out on the image. Reed found another, smaller spot of green in the upper-right-hand corner of the picture. Hoshi zoomed in on that as well.

"A park," she said.

The two of them exchanged puzzled glances.

They found several other patches of silver and green—representing similarly untouched areas of the city—scattered all over the map.

"What is this?" Reed asked. "What are we looking at?"

"The image is of the planet Ondahar VII," Hoshi said, reading off the screen. "We're looking at what was once its capital city, destroyed in a catastrophic explosion that occurred approximately six thousand years ago. According to these records, three hundred thousand people lived in the city at the time of its destruction. Most perished. This image is one of the few surviving records of the Ondahar civilization."

"This has to be some kind of a mistake," Reed said. It looked to him as if someone had taken before and after shots of the city—the attack and its aftermath—and randomly superimposed one on the other.

"No. No mistake." Roan, who had been silent so long Reed almost forgot he was there, leaned forward between the two of them. "I have seen this pattern of destruction before."

"But—there is no pattern," Reed said.

"The energies the Anu'anshee harnessed are not—our scientists said they do not follow the rules of linear space-time. Unleashed, those energies act quixotically. They disperse at random. One building is destroyed—the one next to it survives. A mother might be holding her child's hand one instant—and the next instant, nothing."

"That's hard to imagine."

"The evidence is right here, before your eyes. And I have seen it up close—firsthand. I received burns, and two hundred of my soldiers vanished in an instant."

"This is what happened at Dar Shalaan," Reed guessed.

"That's right," Roan said. "Only on a much larger scale."

Three hundred thousand people had died in the catastrophe on the screen before them. Reed was beginning to rethink his earlier estimate of what sort of powers the Anu'anshee might have been capable of. What their machines were capable of doing. What they had done, perhaps, to Alana.

He thought again of that smell he'd noticed inside the pyramid—ozone, the odor of electricity. But he had seen no machines there, only the stones. And Archer's tricorder readings had revealed nothing either.

So what had happened?

He heard Phlox's voice in his head—

"We need to get back down there," the doctor had said. *"See if we can discover what caused this."*

—and suddenly he saw the doctor, waiting for him just inside the sickbay doors, concern written all over his face.

Eighteen

"LIEUTENANT," PHLOX said. "This way, please."

He led Reed past the diagnostic beds (there was a curtain up around one of them—Alana's, Reed presumed) and into his office. The large monitor above Phlox's desk showed Alana sitting up in one of the diagnostic beds, still in her Starfleet uniform. As Reed watched, she ran her hand along the length of the bed, then touched the diagnostic sensor next to it curiously, as if she'd never seen anything like it before.

The sight brought a smile to his face. When Phlox had called up to the bridge and told him to come to sickbay, Reed had expected the worst.

"She's all right," he said. "Thank God."

"Physically, she is fine. Now that the seizures have stopped."

"The diaphragen did the trick."

"No. By the time I got her back here to sickbay, the diaphragen had ceased working. The seizures had returned—her body temperature was five degrees above normal, elevated heart rate, blood pressure at unsafe levels, muscle fibers were on the point of collapse—" Phlox shook his head. "I was most concerned."

"So what did you do?"

"I did nothing," Phlox said. "They stopped of their own accord."

"I should call the bridge." Reed reached for the com, thinking the captain would be pleased to hear some good news after a day like this one. Archer had sent the lieutenant down on his own—T'Pol had found some references to the Sarkassians in the Vulcan database she wanted to discuss with him.

"That's the good news," Phlox said. "He'll want the bad as well."

Reed froze where he stood, his hand halfway to the switch.

"Go ahead," he told Phlox.

"Ensign Hart appears to have amnesia."

"What?" Of all the things Phlox could have told him were wrong with Alana, that was about the last one Reed expected to hear.

"Amnesia—she's lost her memory. She has no recollection of her life aboard this ship, or her friends, her relatives, the places she's lived—"

"I know what amnesia is, Doctor. I just—I find it surprising that Ensign Hart has it."

"It is not entirely unexpected. The condition is symptomatic of an underlying neurological trauma—as were the seizures."

Reed remembered what Phlox had said back in the shuttlebay, when they'd first returned from the planet's surface:

"Her brain is short-circuiting, and I cannot find the fault in the wiring."

"You couldn't find any trauma before."

"Not with the tricorder, no. However, here in sickbay, using the imaging chamber and noninvasive scanning beams . . . I hoped I would have more success."

"But you didn't."

"No. And I am puzzled as to why—especially given the extent of her memory loss."

"No trauma sounds like good news to me, Doctor." Reed frowned. "Isn't it possible the amnesia was caused by something else?"

"That's not the way memory functions, Lieutenant." Phlox sat down, and pulled his chair close to the desk. "Here. Let me show you."

The doctor keyed in a series of commands, and the image of Hart, still taking in her surroundings, disappeared, to be replaced by a diagram.

"The human brain, Lieutenant. I won't bore you with a detailed lecture on its anatomy, except to say that the cortex," he tapped the topmost portion of the diagram, "is where most of the higher brain functions are consolidated. We are concerned with a portion of the cortex called the hippocampus"—he pointed to the bottom part of the diagram—"which is central to all memory functions. Information taken in by the senses is sent here for cognitive association, and then, if appropriate, passed along elsewhere in the brain for further storage. You may be familiar with the concepts of long- and short-term memory?"

Reed nodded.

"Well, to drastically oversimplify the process—"

"Which I appreciate."

"Short-term memories are stored here"—he pointed to the hippocampus—"and long-term memories, by and large, throughout the cortex."

"What does all this have to do with Ensign Hart?"

"I'm coming to that," Phlox said. He cleared the diagram from his monitor, and Alana reappeared on it. She was standing next to the diagnostic bed, studying the display above it intently as if she'd never seen one before.

Phlox swiveled in the chair to face him.

"First of all, there was apparently no damage to the hippocampus. So her ability to form new memories, to retain information, is intact. Already, in the time since she has awakened, I've seen this process occur. I can't stress how important this is for her long-term prognosis."

"I hear a 'but' coming," Reed said.

"You are correct. The 'but' is the extent of her long-term memory loss. She does not recognize me, or the ship, or pictures of the crew, or her parents, or any images I was able to show her from her past."

"It sounds like she's forgotten everything."

"Yes. Which means you would expect to see massive neurological trauma somewhere in the brain. Perhaps evidence of the electric shock you suggested took place." Phlox shook his head. "It is quite puzzling—and disturbing."

"How so?"

"If there is no damage, Lieutenant, then there is nothing to heal. And that suggests that whatever process has caused this memory loss is not reversible."

"So the memory loss is permanent?"

"I cannot say for sure. The seizures stopped of their own accord. Her memories may spontaneously return as well." Phlox shrugged. "The literature suggests the next forty-eight hours will be critical."

"Can I go in there?" Reed asked, nodding to the monitor. "Talk to her?"

"Ah." Phlox held up a warning finger. "Another problem. Among the things Ensign Hart has lost is the ability to speak."

"She can't talk?"

"No, though I stress that there is nothing physically wrong with her vocal cords. She's simply forgotten how to speak English—which is another puzzling aspect to the injury, as the literature shows that the mapping of declarative and procedural memories is not—"

"Thank you, Doctor," Reed interrupted. "I'll go in now, if that's all right."

"Of course. But Lieutenant—"

"Yes?"

"I know the two of you were close. You may be expecting that seeing you will jog her memory, cause her to come back to herself, as it were. Perhaps it will. But if it doesn't," Phlox's voice hardened here, "please do not react in any sort of negative manner to Ensign Hart—her actions, or lack thereof. Our support and positive reinforcement is vital to her chances of recovery."

"I understand, Doctor," Reed said.

"Good." Phlox turned back to his workstation. He tapped on the keypad again, and the screen filled with the smallest type Reed had ever seen. "You know the way. I'll be here if you need me."

"Thank you, Doctor."

Reed stood at the curtain around Alana's bed, and pulled it gently aside—just enough to peek in and watch her.

Alana was lying down on the bed again, staring up at the ceiling. Brow furrowed, eyes half-closed, concentrating intently. It was the same old

Alana he was seeing, looking just the way she had during those first few firing drills in the armory, when she was trying to work the kinks out of her reflexes. To remember the way her body used to work. The thought made him optimistic. All the things she'd forgotten—the names, the people, the places—they might all come back to her just as easily.

He drew the curtain wide, and cleared his throat. "Excuse me."

At the sound of his voice, she started, and looked up quickly. Their eyes locked.

At that instant, Reed realized that he was completely wrong—it wasn't the same old Alana at all.

The person sitting on the diagnostic bed was someone else entirely—a total stranger to him. Someone who had no memory at all of their relationship, someone who didn't know him from Adam or any other person on the ship. Someone who, right now, regarded him with only suspicion and alarm.

He remembered what Phlox had said, and forced the smile to remain frozen on his face.

"I'm sorry," he said. "I don't know how much of what I say you can understand—I didn't mean to startle you. My name is Malcolm Reed."

Her expression remained guarded. He took a step forward, hesitantly.

"Can I come in—talk with you a moment?"

She sat up suddenly. The movement startled

him—not so much because of its speed, but the way she did it. Totally unlike any way he'd ever seen Alana move, as if she'd forgotten the way her body worked.

"I'm glad to see you're better. You had us all worried."

Her expression remained suspicious.

"You and I," he said, pointing first to himself, then her. "We were good friends. We worked together—in the armory."

She stared at him curiously a moment.

"Armory," she said hesitantly.

"That's right." Reed smiled at her. "Armory. Good."

She smiled back.

It looked forced, unnatural. As if the expression was somehow completely alien to her.

Reed felt his own smile waver then, and cleared his throat, searching for something to say.

Far off in the distance, he thought he heard the com sound. He turned to answer it.

But there was no com on the wall next to him.

The room around him wavered, like an incoming transmission suddenly disrupted by static, and disappeared.

He took a step back, and wobbled on his feet.

Nineteen

"LIEUTENANT REED? ARE YOU ALL RIGHT?"

He blinked, and suddenly he was back in the lab, with Roan staring at him curiously. Hoshi turned in her chair to look at him as well, concern on her face.

Being in sickbay, with Alana again—that was just another memory, shooting to the surface of his mind. More intense than before though—as if whatever mechanism was prompting these recollections was increasing in urgency. He should go see Phlox, tell him about it. And he would.

After.

"Malcolm?" Hoshi asked.

"I'm fine," he said, trying not to sound snappish and—he suspected—failing. "Just a little tired."

The com sounded again.

"Repeat, T'Pol to Lieutenant Reed. Lieutenant, are you there?"

He crossed the room and opened a channel.

"Right here, Sub-Commander."

"Commodore Roan is with you?"

"He is. We're going through the archives."

"We need you in launch bay two now. We are ready to proceed."

"The binary star provides us with our window of opportunity," T'Pol said. "As the two stars approach perihelion—their closest distance to each other—there is a flare-up of radiation across the EM spectrum, lasting approximately two hours. This should create a pattern of interference strong enough that their sensors will be unable to register the shuttlepod's approach."

The captain and she stood with Reed and Roan in launch bay two. Behind the four of them, two crewmen from engineering were preparing Shuttlepod One for launch.

"I understand that part," Roan said. "Perhaps I'm not making myself clear. The outpost is not that large. Even if their sensors don't detect us, there is a good chance they will simply see the shuttlepod landing."

"We are taking all possible steps to minimize that occurrence," T'Pol said. She handed Reed her padd. "You'll see the course I've plotted for you, Lieutenant."

Reed studied the small screen. T'Pol's course called for the pod to come in on the far side of the planetoid and skim the surface at what would have been treetop level on Earth, finally using the pyramid as cover to land at the outpost.

"You should have enough time to return Commodore Roan to the planet—and to retrieve the necessary records."

"It's risky—there's no denying it," the captain said. "But we've got a little bit of a distraction planned as well."

"Sir?"

"We're going to make a show of trying to break through their jamming beam. Nothing extreme, mind you," he said, off Reed's look of concern, "just enough of a sustained effort that the ambassador notices."

Levy, one of the crewmen preparing the pod, stepped forward. "Excuse me, sirs. We're all set."

"Thank you, Crewman," the captain said. "Well, Malcolm, Commodore—you'd better get aboard."

T'Pol checked her tricorder. "Indeed. Perihelion in seven minutes."

Roan turned to Archer. "I want you to know again how much I appreciate what you have done for me, Captain. And my people."

"Our pleasure. The next time our two races meet, Commodore, I want it to be as friends." Archer handed Roan a small sample container. "And here is a token of our friendship."

Roan opened the container. "The *phondrikaar.*"

"It's yours . . . as promised."

"Thank you, Captain."

The two men shook hands.

"I appreciate your efforts as well, Sub-Commander," Roan said, turning to T'Pol.

"I wish you luck, Commodore," T'Pol said. "Live long and prosper."

"I plan on doing both—thanks to you, and your doctor. Please don't forget to convey my regards to him as well."

"Of course."

"One last thing, Lieutenant," T'Pol said. "There is a downside to the interference we are counting on to mask your descent. It will also—more than likely—prevent you from communicating with us once perihelion occurs."

Reed shrugged. "I don't see where we'll have much to talk about, sirs. Fly down, drop off the commodore, pick up the records, and fly back. That's all there is, isn't it?"

"That's all." The captain took a step closer to Reed. "Malcolm, I've already lost one crewman on this mission. I do not want to lose a second."

"No, sir."

"No matter what happens down there—if you find the records or not—you make that launch window. Get out while the interference is still strong enough to mask your takeoff. Is that understood?"

"Yes, sir," Reed said.

"Good man." Archer clapped him on the shoulder. "We'll see you shortly."

"Aye, sir. Commodore—shall we?"

He gestured toward the open shuttlepod door. With a final nod to Archer and T'Pol, Roan entered the small craft.

Reed took a last look around the launch bay himself. The mission was as simple as he'd outlined it. In two hours—approximately—he'd be back aboard *Enterprise,* safe and sound.

Approximately, he realized.

There was that word again.

Reed sat in the pilot's chair. He gave the commodore control of weapons, on the off chance that they'd need them. On that off chance, he even started explaining how the various systems aboard the pod functioned.

But once they'd dropped out of orbit to the planetoid's surface, he had to stop talking and concentrate on piloting the ship. Because there was another complicating factor to the mission T'Pol had forgotten to mention.

The interference not only made it impossible for them to communicate with *Enterprise,* but also rendered their sensors virtually useless.

Which would not normally have been a problem, given that the planetoid was airless and visibility was excellent. He'd done dozens of similar landings, without instruments, relying solely on the naked eye to make his approach and bring his ship down.

Only in this case, he didn't have to just bring his ship down; he had to guide it halfway around the planetoid at a height of one hundred meters. And the problem with that, he quickly realized, was that the asteroid was rocky, and there were lots of other things that occupied that same one-hundred-meter height he was flying at. Reed didn't know whether to call them crags, or outcrops, or hills, or mountains, or what-have-yous—and it didn't really matter. He had to dodge them all without going too high above the hundred-meter ceiling—it was like an old-fashioned roller-coaster ride.

Finally it ended, though, and the pod touched down in the shadow of the pyramid.

Minutes later, they accessed the tunnel complex, and emerged into one of the modules Roan had been using as part of his temporary base camp. They were, Reed realized, exactly the same kind of modules he and Trip and Bishop had noticed on the planet's surface—larger on the inside than Reed would have expected for such simple structures.

The interior of the one Roan had guided him to was a ruin.

"They have been here. Valay, and her forces." He strode quickly to a cabinet on the far side of the room and threw it open.

The inside was a charred mass of plastic and metal. Reed could smell it from where he stood.

"This is where we found the outpost's records—what the scientists had discovered down here." He shook his head. "Why would she do this?"

"So what we're looking for . . ."

"Is gone. Everything is gone. It makes no sense." Roan looked around the module's interior, and his eyes lit on what looked to Reed like a computer terminal. He crossed quickly to it, and flipped a series of switches.

"Dead as well. The raw data was in here—I thought we could give that to you, at least, even if . . ." He sighed. "I am sorry, Lieutenant. I will have to send you back empty-handed."

Reed stood there, and all he could think of was Alana. What would happen to her memory if he left the outpost now, and returned to *Enterprise*.

He couldn't do it.

"I can't go back yet, sir. I need to find out what happened to her. To my friend."

"And I wish I could help you do that. But the records simply aren't here."

"Commodore, you don't understand. Starfleet is going to convene a hearing on her behavior, and no matter what I believe, or what the captain believes, she's going to be found guilty—of insanity at the very least. Possibly court-martialed, her name tarnished . . ." He shook his head. "We have to go back in to the pyramid, and see if we can find out what happened there."

"To the pyramid? Lieutenant . . ." Roan shook his head. "You heard what your captain said. I heard what your captain said. If the records weren't here, you're to get back to the ship."

"No, that's not what he said. He said I had to make that launch window, and according to T'Pol's estimates," Reed glanced at his tricorder, "I still have an hour and twenty minutes to do that. Plenty of time to reach the pyramid and take readings."

"I promise you, Lieutenant. I will take readings for you—later. Once the situation with Valay is resolved. It is simply too dangerous for you to stay down here a minute more."

"I'm not asking for your permission," Reed said. "Or your help. I know where the central chamber is. I know how to get to the pyramid from it. You do what you need to."

They'd come up into the module by climbing a ladder. Now he put his foot on the topmost rung, and started to climb back down, realizing as he went that without the environmental suit, he'd be able to move much faster than previously. He should have time enough not only to retrace his steps to the place he'd found Alana, but possibly even explore the interior further.

"Wait."

Reed looked up the ladder, and saw Roan's face peering over the edge.

"You're being foolhardy, you know."

Reed sighed. He didn't have time to even begin an explanation of his actions to Roan. More than ever, he was certain that the answers he was looking for lay back in the pyramid, back where he'd found Alana. Roan's answers were there too, he felt. Why Valay had acted as she had, done the things she'd done . . .

"Completely out of character," the commodore had called her behavior, Reed recalled.

And suddenly Reed realized he and Roan were both dealing with the same question—what could cause someone to change so completely? Because Valay was different now from the first time he'd seen her, in just as dramatic a way as Alana had been different after she'd returned from the planet.

Reed paused on the ladder a moment, remembering.

Twenty

"IT'S NOT THE COMMODORE." Hoshi listened to the com traffic on her earpiece and frowned. "Different source altogether."

Archer swiveled in his chair to face Hoshi. "But it is the Sarkassians?"

"Yes," she said.

"The signal is coming over subspace frequencies from a point outside the Eris Alpha system." T'Pol looked up from her viewer. "They are using a series of satellite relays to disguise the transmission's origin."

"They don't want us to know where they're from," Archer said.

"Hardly surprising," Reed added. "Wouldn't expect them to put out the welcome mat after how they've acted so far."

236

"Let's see what they want." Archer nodded to Hoshi. "Put it up onscreen."

The viewer filled with the image of a Sarkassian female. Her skin was the same pale white as Roan's, her hair long and streaked with crimson, held back from her face by a simple purple band. She wore a long robe of the same color, and stood in the middle of an ornate chamber made of what looked like floor-to-ceiling panes of colored glass.

"Earth vessel *Enterprise,* this is Ambassador Valay Shuma aboard the *Striker Amileus.* Your presence in our space is an act of aggression."

"So we've been told, Ambassador," the captain said.

"You are Archer?"

"Yes, and as I've tried to explain, we were responding to a distress call—"

"Archer, we are en route to your position now, estimated arrival time approximately nine hours," the ambassador interrupted. "We will hear your explanation at that time."

"That's Captain Archer, if you don't mind, Ambassador. And we were made aware of your coming and your arrival time earlier. Is there another purpose to this communication?"

"Yes. We have tentatively identified the man you currently hold aboard your ship."

The screen suddenly filled with the image of the alien they'd brought back from the outpost, lying in his bed in sickbay. For a second Reed wondered how the Sarkassians had obtained it—then remembered the image Phlox had provided to Roan.

"According to our records, he is Mercantor Gol, a crewman on the *Relayer Haven*—a shuttle recently sent to resupply the outpost. You may be aware that it was the *Haven*'s crash into the outpost that resulted in the death of our scientists."

"We knew something had destroyed your atmospheric containment field. We didn't know what."

"It was the *Haven*," Valay said. "We have just finished reconstructing the incident. There was an explosion aboard the craft just prior to landing. The pilot lost control."

"Sounds like your crewman here was lucky to survive."

"He is not our crewman," Valay said. "And we believe his survival had nothing to do with luck."

Reed and the captain exchanged a puzzled look.

"I'm sorry," Archer said. "You've lost me."

"Mercantor Gol did not exist until six months ago. This so-called survivor you rescued is an impostor."

The image from sickbay vanished, and was replaced by another. A man standing in front of a very familiar-looking building, a virtual twin of the one Reed and Trip had explored while at the outpost. He was dressed in some sort of uniform. Arms folded across his chest, he stood in front of the building as if determined to defend it to the death.

"We believe he is actually this man—Kostal Goridian. We further believe he deliberately caused the explosion aboard the shuttle, in order to destroy our facility."

Reed studied the image carefully. There was a slight facial resemblance between this Goridian and the man they had in sickbay, but Goridian seemed far closer to human than Sarkassian—his build was stockier, his skin color darker . . . even the proportions of his limbs seemed different.

But it could be the same man. And if it was . . .

Being found next to Alana could hardly be a co-incidence. He must have had something to do with what happened to her.

Valay reappeared on the viewer.

"The purpose of our call is to urge you to take extreme caution when dealing with Goridian. He is capable of anything."

"Why would he do this?" Archer asked.

"He is Ta'alaat. We are at war with his people."

"But the man in our sickbay is—or appears to be—Sarkassian."

"*Appears* is the correct word, Captain. There are ways of altering one's appearance. Goridian is master of all of them—and a very dangerous man. Please prepare him for immediate transport to Commodore Roan's ship."

Archer was silent a moment.

"Ambassador, we had a crewperson injured down on the planetoid's surface. If this Goridian is who you say he is, I will want to question him about that."

"We will be happy to share what relevant information we glean from him with you," Valay said.

Archer nodded thoughtfully. Reed would have bet money the captain's thoughts mirrored his own—based on the way the Sarkassians had acted so far, once *Enterprise* transferred Goridian to Roan's vessel, they would never see him again.

"Very well," Archer said. "Of course, any talk of transferring the prisoner now is premature. He is still unconscious, after all. And I'm sure our doctor would not want us to move him in this condition."

"I see." Valay's eyes were like pinpricks. "Very well, Captain. Until our arrival, you may maintain custody of the prisoner. As I said, however, he is extremely dangerous. Do you have confinement facilities aboard your ship?"

Archer turned to Reed.

"We can make do, sir," Reed said. In fact, *Enterprise* had a brig, but he was in the middle of reconfiguring it entirely, to try and incorporate what they'd learned about forcefield technology over the last year into its design. It would be simple enough to construct something temporary, though, that one prisoner would have no chance of escaping.

"We'll be able to put the prisoner into a secure environment," Archer told Valay.

"Very well," she said. "Until tomorrow."

The screen went dark.

"I must warn you again, Captain, of the dangers involved in interfering in a conflict between these two races," T'Pol said. "We cannot be seen to be taking sides. Keeping this prisoner away from the Sarkassians is a dangerous act."

"I want to know what happened to Ensign Hart," Archer said. "Beyond that, who has the prisoner and what happens to him doesn't concern me." Archer turned to Reed. "You'll get to work on that brig, Malcolm?"

"Aye, sir."

"Another transmission coming through from the ambassador's ship, sir," Hoshi said.

Archer nodded. "Put it up."

"It's not audio, sir. It's a data burst."

"Decoding now," T'Pol said. "It appears to be a biographical dossier on this Goridian."

"Send a copy down to sickbay, Sub-Commander," Archer said. "Let the doctor have a look at it."

"Aye, sir."

Reed punched in a series of instructions to the computer to send a copy of the file to his system as well. When the prisoner woke, Reed wanted to be prepared with some questions of his own.

He ordered Bishop to the bridge, and then got to work.

They set up the brig in an unfinished cabin on C-deck. It took several hours—Reed spent most of that time there, supervising and, increasingly, pitching in. The work was physical, and by the time it was finished, he was sweating, and he was hungry, and most of all, he was tired.

But eating and showering could wait. He wanted to see Alana.

He made his way to sickbay, on a sudden impulse stopping in her quarters first. He found Phlox in his lab, bent over a microscope.

"Doctor?"

Phlox looked up, and Reed saw that the doctor was several shades paler than usual.

"What's the matter?"

"A most unsettling experience," Phlox said. "This alien—the one you brought back from the outpost? I've just discovered he brought a nasty virus on board with him. I was just examining it—an incredibly hardy little beast. Tough to kill—and very deadly. Lethal across almost all species lines, as far as I can tell."

Reed froze in his tracks.

"Good lord." His mind raced through the biowarfare protocol—quarantine, decontamination, neutralization. "I'll contact the captain—let him know we should close down the areas of the ship the alien was in, initiate—"

"There's no need for that, Lieutenant," Phlox said. "I did not mean to worry you unnecessarily. I have already destroyed the virus—all except this one sample, which, since I have now committed its basic structure to our data banks," Phlox pressed a button next to the microscope, and a brief flash of ultraviolet light flared, "can be safely destroyed as well."

"The alien brought that on board with him?"

Phlox nodded. "Concealed inside a vial in the heel of one of his shoes. I also found several other concealed weapons, inside his clothing—and his body."

"His body?"

"His teeth. Underneath his fingernails. Elsewhere."

"It seems the ambassador was right, then," Reed said, almost to himself. "This man was behind the attack on the outpost. He's not Sarkassian."

"I have no baseline readings to compare his with," Phlox said. "But there are a number of drugs in his system which are masking certain phenotypical characteristics. Skin color, for one. Hair thickness, body odor—I can't be entirely certain what other functions the drugs have."

"But he's in disguise?"

"Oh yes."

"And still unconscious?"

"Not just unconscious. Here. Let me show you." Phlox shut off the microscope, and turned on his workstation. The image of the alien, lying on one of the diagnostic beds, filled the screen. "He is in a deep coma—though perhaps *coma* is the wrong word, as my instruments reveal almost no indication of higher brain function." Phlox frowned. "Of course, there is the possibility that in his species, neural activity is not based on the same biochemical reactions as ours."

"I'm more concerned with whether or not he's going to wake up and present an active danger to the ship."

"I understand. On that matter, I have no way of knowing."

Reed studied the prisoner—Goridian—for a moment. He saw that the security straps on the bed had been fastened. That was good.

But not good enough, he decided, remembering the destruction they'd seen at the outpost, the weapons Phlox found, and what the ambassador had said to him earlier:

"Take extreme caution when dealing with Goridian. He is capable of anything."

"I want to move him to the brig we've set up—now," Reed said. "Will that present a problem for you?"

Phlox hesitated only a second. "No. Not as long as I can continue to monitor his condition. It will be necessary to install a tie-in to my systems here."

"Shouldn't be a problem. I'll have Mister Bishop down here in a minute." Reed hesitated a moment. "Doctor. Alana—Ensign Hart. How's she doing?"

Now Phlox smiled. "See for yourself," he said, and the image on the monitor changed to one of Hart, sitting up in another of the diagnostic beds.

She was reading.

Reed smiled as well. "That's—incredible."

"It is astounding. In less than twelve hours, she has managed to reacquire a working knowledge of the English language."

"What's she reading?"

Phlox consulted the monitor. "Technical documents relating to the armory."

"She wants to get back to work."

"I suspect you are correct. However, that would not be a good idea."

"Why? You think the seizures might return?"

"No. My concern at the moment is not with her physical recovery, but her mental well-being."

Reed frowned. "The fact that she's trying so hard to relearn what she's forgotten—isn't that a positive sign?"

"Yes. But I wish she would express as much concern about recovering the personal details of her life. Who she was, rather than simply what she did."

"Perhaps I can help her with that aspect of things."

"Perhaps you can," Phlox said.

Reed frowned. "I hear a 'but' in there."

"Yes. No." Phlox frowned. "I am sure it's just an instrument error."

"Doctor? What are you talking about?"

"Some readings I took. As I said, it's not important."

"It's clearly bothering you, though." Reed folded his arms across his chest. "Come on, Doctor. Tell me."

"Well." Phlox nodded. "All right. Like the ensign, I too have been reading. A bit far afield from the usual medical journals. Prompted by our discussion yesterday, as a matter of fact."

"Go on."

Phlox swiveled in his chair. "We were talking about memory loss," he said, and cleared the screen again. An article appeared—one with very small print.

Reed peered over the Doctor's shoulder and read the title.

" 'Measuring Quantum States Within Bioelectric Organisms.' " He had to laugh. "Our conversation prompted you to read this?"

"In a way. The article is several years old—among other things, it talks about the most challenging problem facing scientists who were then trying to build the transporter. That being, the successful measurement and replication of the complex web of electromagnetic fields associated with the human brain."

Reed frowned. "What does this have to do with the readings you're talking about?"

"I'm coming to that." Phlox cleared the screen again, and a diagnostic chart filled it.

"This is Ensign Hart's EEG—a measurement of the electrical activity in her brain. I regularly take EEGs from all the crew for their physicals. This one is from six months ago. And this"—he keyed in a few commands to the computer, and the screen split in half—"is an EEG I took this morning."

"They're different."

"Very different."

Reed frowned. "Isn't that to be expected—given what's happened to her?"

"Not to this degree—at least, not in my experience. Furthermore, the human brain is not the only part of the body that generates electricity. All cells produce it, as a part of their day-to-day functioning. I take readings of that activity as well. Taken in combination with the EEG, these readings produce a characteristic electromagnetic field—one that is specific to each individual. Some scientists believe that the essence of personality itself is contained within these fields— what makes us individuals."

He put another set of readings up on the screen.

"Before the accident"—Phlox said, pointing to the chart on the left—"and after it," he continued, pointing to the chart on the right.

"Different as well."

"Completely different—which is impossible, of course. Which is why I'm reconstructing her medical file to compare these results with the ones taken while she was aboard *Achilles.*"

"Reconstructing?"

"Our older medical archives have been archived in preparation for our rendezvous with the *Shi'ar,*" Phlox said. "It's taking quite some time for the system to find and extract Ensign Hart's records."

Reed shook his head. He didn't completely see where Phlox was going with this. "What does all this have to do with memory loss?"

"I'm not sure yet," Phlox said thoughtfully. He cleared the screen. "These readings are indicative of the kind of neural damage I was looking for yesterday—though it's more a reconstructive process, a rewiring of critical pathways, than the destructive tissue loss I would have expected to see. But in either case," he sighed, "it tells me that Ensign Hart's memory loss is more than likely permanent."

"I see," Reed said. "What happened to the forty-eight-hour window you were talking about yesterday?"

"We're in it now. And I see no signs of any recovery." His eyes found Reed's. "I'm sorry, Lieutenant."

"There's still hope though—isn't there?"

"Well." Phlox smiled. "There's always hope."

"Then let me get in there," Reed said. "And see what I can do."

* * *

"Hello."

Alana turned away from the monitor quickly.

"Hello. Lieutenant Reed."

Reed couldn't hide his surprise. Her English was letter-perfect—a slight accent that she hadn't had before, but he chalked that up to whatever language tapes she'd used.

"You remember me?"

"Yes. From yesterday."

"That's good," he said, moving closer. Alana was wearing one of the standard-issue sickbay gowns now instead of her uniform. Her hair was pulled up underneath a cap. The gown was loose—too big perhaps, or maybe it was just the way she was wearing it, but it made her look small, and frail, and vulnerable.

It made him want to hold her, to touch her.

Instead, he put the Corbett facsimile on the cot next to her.

"What is this?" she asked.

"It's a book," he said. "One of yours. We both were rather fond of it."

"England in the Seven Years' War." She frowned. "What is England?"

"It's a country on Earth," he said. "Actually, the country where I come from. Alana, look at this book closely, please. Do you remember it at all?"

He turned the pages slowly for her, one at a time. Many of them were crinkled at the edges, from the night her drink had spilled. He watched her eyes as she studied it, hoping for a flicker of recognition.

She only shook her head.

"This is from a long time ago," she said. "It is not important."

"It's more about strategy. How England was able to win such a long war."

She shook her head. "Seven years is not a long war."

With a sigh, Reed closed the book. "I suppose not, but—"

She looked up at him. "I was in war. The doctor said I was a soldier."

"Well." Reed smiled. "A little more than a soldier, I think."

"And that I worked here." She swiveled the monitor around so that Reed could see it. She was looking at a series of blueprints from the armory—the torpedo bays, the weapons lockers, the firing console.

"Yes," he said.

"I am ready to work again."

"You will," he said gently. "But let's take things one step at a time. Make sure you're all better first."

"I am all better. I am all fine."

He smiled at her awkward construction of the language—she may have mastered the form, but she had a long ways to go before the idiom came back to her.

"Now is not the time for you to go back on

duty," he said firmly. "We're in the middle of a very—complicated situation."

"The Sarkassians."

Reed couldn't keep the surprise off his face.

"Yes—how did you know about them?"

She pointed to the workstation next to her. "This. The Sarkassians. The *Shi'ar.* I know."

"Then I don't have to explain. There's not time to—to help you remember the things we do. We have to concentrate on the Sarkassians—make sure nothing goes wrong." He smiled. "We don't want that, do we?"

"No," she said after a moment's pause. "We don't want that."

He nodded. "That's right. You can't rush things. The Doctor wants to—and I want to—help you remember more about the past—not just what you used to do in the armory, but who you used to be. Your family, your friends . . ."

Impulsively, he reached out for her hand, and took it.

It was cold to the touch.

He looked up and found her eyes. They were cold as well.

In that instant, his heart sank. Phlox was right, he knew it then. The person lying on the cot before him—

It wasn't Alana.

Alana was gone.

And she wasn't coming back.

Twenty-One

ROAN HAD INSISTED ON COMING with him ("To make sure you get back safely") and nothing Reed said could convince him otherwise.

He set a brisk pace, one that the commodore was barely able to match. By the time they reached the area where he'd found Alana, Roan was breathing heavily.

"We're here." Reed knelt down, running one hand along the ground. A thin layer of dirt coated the pyramid floor—he saw scuff marks where she had lain. "This is the place."

They explored the area, and everything around it for fifty yards in all directions. No signs of any sort of machinery. Nothing on the tricorder, either.

Nothing but the stones, standing still and silent all around them.

"Grave markers," Roan said suddenly.

"I beg your pardon?"

"That is what these stones remind me of. Some of the other, more primitive cultures we have encountered—they dig holes in the ground and put their dead into them. Then they mark the location of those holes with markers. Such as these."

"Tombstones," Reed said. "That's what we call them."

"Excuse me?"

"The markers we use—tombstones." Reed shrugged. "I hate to place us among your more primitive cultures, but we often bury our dead as well."

"Why?"

"It provides us with a place to go—to be with the people who died. To remember them."

"We cremate our dead—after harvesting all the usable organs. If we want to remember them, we have their images. Their words."

"As do we, but—I've found there is a difference," Reed said. "Having some place to go—set aside specifically for those memories."

Roan nodded thoughtfully. "Yes. Perhaps 'primitive' was the wrong way to describe such habits."

Both were silent a moment. Reed forced his thoughts away from burial customs, and back to the problem at hand—what had happened to Alana. He walked back over to the spot where he'd first found her, and thought.

Goridian had booby-trapped the tunnel for them—or rather, for the Sarkassians, whom he'd been expecting to come after him. Had he set another trap here as well—one that Alana had triggered? One whose effects he had miscalculated, knocking himself unconscious in the bargain?

Or had Alana accidentally set something off that got the both of them? Or retriggered a device that had already hurt Goridian? If so, where was it?

His head spun with questions. He spun slowly in a circle, scanning the area yet again. Nothing.

He walked back over to Roan, lips pursed in frustration.

"Damm it," he said. "There must be something here that could have—"

Roan had his arms folded behind his back, hands clasped together. He was staring back in the direction they'd come from, his eyes glistening.

"Sir?"

The commodore blinked, and sighed heavily.

"Are you all right?"

"Just—thinking, Lieutenant. About burial customs. The Ta'alaat use grave markers as well. Seeing all these"—he waved at the stones spread out before them—"I'm reminded of those who died at Dar Shalaan. Though there were no bodies, there, of course. They had to construct a monument."

"Commodore—what happened there?"

"It is the same story I have told you before—up to a point, of course. Twenty years ago, within

254

one of the Ta'alaat temples, we discovered an energy source of enormous power. By this point, we were more sensitive to the Ta'alaat's concerns. We continued to allow them access to the site for the majority of each day, permitting our scientists to work only during the night hours. Neither side was happy with the arrangement, but—we thought it a fair compromise.

"Ta'alaat extremists did not, apparently. They struck during the night, killing our scientists, and occupying the temple. I was ordered to lead the counterstrike—to make an example of them." Roan shook his head. "Actually, that's not entirely correct. I volunteered to lead the counterstrike.

"Something we did in the attack—it caused the power source to explode. I remember—one minute, I was standing on a hill, overlooking the battle, in the midst of my troops. In the next . . . everything was gone. I was one of the lucky ones, to escape with these burns." Roan shook his head. "It was a turning point in our history, needless to say. All official contacts between our peoples were severed. A turning point for me, as well. There were those among us who had all along fought to change our policy toward the Ta'alaat. I joined them then, hoping to perhaps make a difference. To make up for what I'd done."

It was Reed's turn to be silent a moment.

He thought of Alana—the guilt she'd felt over

killing two Vulcan hostages by accident. It had tormented her all her life.

Multiply that guilt by a factor of—what, a hundred thousand? It was inconceivable. He couldn't even begin to imagine what Roan felt.

But it at least gave him some insight into why the commodore was so determined to continue his fight.

Reed checked his tricorder. Ten minutes had passed. Fifty-five minutes left in his launch window.

"We still have some time, Commodore. I'd like to enlarge the search area, see if we can't—"

Something made a sound behind him. Reed turned.

Ambassador Valay emerged from behind one of the stones. Two men stepped out with her.

"I'm afraid time is what you no longer have, gentlemen."

Reed had reached for his phase pistol the instant he'd heard a noise. The grip in his hand, he started to raise it and fire—

And saw that the two men with Valay both held weapons, pointed straight at him and the Commodore.

He lowered his.

"Good," Valay said. "But better to drop it entirely—in my direction."

He did as she asked. Valay picked up the pistol, not taking her eyes off him the entire time.

Roan had turned a split second after Reed. Now he faced Valay, and the others, and his eyes widened in surprise.

"Kellan? Ash? You're with her?"

"After what you have done?" The man who'd spoken took another step forward, the gun in his hand shaking. His anger was palpable. "You dare ask that?"

"What I've done?" He glared at Valay. "Kellan, what lies has she been telling you?"

"That you had made cause with the humans—sold them the secrets of our technology in exchange for money."

"It is a lie."

"We have been tracking you since you landed," Kellan said. "You took this man to the scientists' quarters, and then here."

Reed frowned. They hadn't picked up any sign at all of the ambassador's ship leaving orbit.

And all of a sudden he knew why. The *phondrikaar.* Valay's ship was a Striker—Roan had said that material, impervious to their sensors, had been incorporated into the hulls of all such ships.

"I have fought for Sarkassia for all my life—you think I could ever betray us?" Roan asked. "Reed is here only because he wants to find out what happened to his crewman, and I agreed to—"

"What is this, then?" Valay asked.

She held up the small storage container that Roan had set down on the ground next to him.

Reed's heart leapt into his mouth.

The *phondrikaar*.

She opened the container, and held up its contents for the others to see.

"I think Kellan can tell who has our people's interest at heart, Commodore," Valay said.

"No!" Roan said. "This is not what it seems—they are returning this material to us. Lieutenant Reed will verify that."

Reed nodded. "He's telling the truth."

"Do you take us all for fools? Of course you're returning the *phondrikaar*—now that you've finished studying it." Valay shook her head. "Butcher is no longer the appropriate name to cover your crimes. We must add another one, Commodore. Traitor."

"I am no traitor," Roan said. "Let us contact the Executive Council, and see who the traitor is."

"And in times of war," Valay continued, ignoring him, "there is only one penalty for traitors."

She held up the phase pistol.

And then, to Reed's astonishment, she adjusted the setting on the weapon. As expertly, as naturally, as if she'd been trained on it.

Reed stared at her in open-mouthed surprise. There was no way she could know how to do that. How—

Valay raised the weapon again and fired.

The beam struck Roan square in the chest, and the Commodore vanished in a haze of energy.

"Commodore!" Reed cried, taking a step forward.

"Stop."

Reed looked up to see Kellan pointing his weapon directly at him.

"Stay where you are."

Valay turned to him.

"Under Sarkassian law," she said. "The penalty for those who collaborate in an act of treason is the same."

She raised the phase pistol again.

Reed tensed.

What was it they said was supposed to happen before you died? Your life flashed before your eyes?

He waited.

And then, as if coming from far off in the distance, he heard Trip's voice, echoing in his mind.

Twenty-Two

ARMORY
1/15/2151 0110 HOURS

"WHY DON'T YOU DRAG A COT in, at least?"

Reed was staring at the firing console. He looked up and saw Trip standing in the door to the armory, framed by the dim lights of the corridor behind him. He hadn't even heard the door open.

"I'm sorry, sir, but I don't believe this is your department."

"Har har." Trip stepped inside, and the door slid shut behind him. "You know what time it is?"

"About one."

"About a little after one. What are you doing that's so all-fired important it can't wait till morning?"

"My job."

"Meaning—"

"Meaning I don't like being sandwiched in between two enemy ships waiting for a third to show up and leave us even more outgunned."

"So—"

"So I'm using some of the data we picked up from sensor readings to run a few combat simulations—just in case."

"So how we doin'?"

"Not well—yet." Which was an understatement—in all the scenarios Reed had run, *Enterprise* only managed to inflict minimal damage to one of the Sarkassian ships before the others ganged up and destroyed her. "I've got some ideas, though."

"I've got some ideas, too," Trip said. "Number one being, there's a reason they call 'em ambassadors, and not soldiers. You know what I'm saying? Valay—as obnoxious as she might sound—is coming to talk, not to fight."

"Just covering all the bases," Reed said. "As I mentioned—it is my job."

"Your department's job," Trip said. "Where's everyone else?"

"Santini's on station on the bridge. Everyone else is asleep."

"Ah-hah."

"Don't worry, Trip. I'll be joining them soon enough."

"All right then."

Reed entered a few more variables into the simulation. He wished he knew more about the Sarkassian ship's capabilities at impulse—

how much power their weapons drew off the warp engines, and how dependent they were on that.

When he looked up, Trip was still standing there. "What?"

"Been meaning to ask you," his friend said quietly, in a different tone of voice altogether. "How's Hart?"

She's dead, Reed started to say.

Except she wasn't. Not yet. This was the past. And he was—

Down on the outpost. Inside the pyramid.

Valay held the phase pistol on him, a thoughtful expression on her face.

"Not with this," she said, and lowered the weapon.

He blinked, and he was back in the armory, Trip standing next to him, looking over his shoulder at the console monitor.

"That didn't work either," he said, pointing at the screen, as *Enterprise* was destroyed again in yet another combat simulation. "What else you got up your sleeve?"

Reed stood stock-still a moment, not answering.

This was just a memory—a moment in time he was reliving. But he'd never experienced anything like this before, never recalled the past with this kind of intensity in his life. Sleep deprivation was not an excuse for these kinds of hallucinations. Something was happening to him. Something that had to do with the change that had come over Alana, and Valay, and the secrets hidden inside the Sarkassian outpost.

He heard the door behind him open, and looked up.

Trip was gone.

Alana stood in the doorway.

His heart sank. He knew where he was, when he was, and what was about to happen next. And nothing he could do would change it.

He had to relive the next few moments, like a prisoner in his own body.

"What are you doing here?" he asked. "What are you doing awake, for that matter?"

She looked surprised to see him as well.

"I wanted to see the armory," she said.

She was still wearing her gown from sickbay.

"Phlox didn't let you out, did he?"

She didn't answer him, just stepped forward into the room, one hand held behind her, as if she was hiding something.

The door hissed shut behind her.

Reed shook his head. "You wanted to see the armory, now you've seen it. Now you've got to get back to sickbay, Alana, you're not—"

He was perhaps four feet away when she took her hand out from behind her back.

She was holding a metal pipe—or a piece of metal that looked like a pipe, something perhaps a foot long, an inch thick . . .

Tubing from the diagnostic cot? Or—

She lunged forward, and caught him square across the head with it.

He staggered back, she swung again, and caught him on the head again.

Reed collapsed on the floor, and lay there a moment, stunned.

Blood trickled down his face.

Alana walked past him, heading toward the firing console.

His head pounded. His vision swam—but through the haze, he saw the lights on the console flicker in an all-too-familiar pattern, and realized instantly what Alana was doing.

She was bringing *Enterprise*'s weapons on-line.

"Don't," he mumbled, trying to get to his feet, and failing.

His vision swam.

Inside the pyramid, Valay turned to Kellan.

"Give me your weapon," she said.

Reed swayed on his feet. His head reeled. Past and present, memory and reality, were all merging together into one.

"Ambassador?" Kellan said hesitantly. "Why—"

"Lieutenant, give me your weapon," Valay commanded. "Now."

Kellan lowered his arm, and turned toward her.

Now, Reed thought. Jump him. Now, you can—

He was in the armory, on his hands and knees.

Alana had charged the ship's weapons. It was madness. The Sarkassians would see that, and charge theirs. They were seconds away from a catastrophic battle. And then, almost certainly—

An even more catastrophic war.

"Stop," he shouted, but it came out as no more than a mumble again. "Alana, stop!"

She paid no attention to him.

Reed groaned, and tried to crawl forward. The firing console was fifty feet away from him. Too far, he realized instantly. He'd never make it.

The com blared.

"Bridge to armory, report. O'Neill to Reed, report! What is happening? Why have you charged weapons?"

Weapons, Reed realized. The weapons lockers were right behind him.

Reed turned, and pried open the nearest one. A phase pistol case, bright metallic blue, about the size of an old-fashioned ledger, tumbled onto the floor. He popped open the case and pulled out one of the phase pistols, and set it to stun.

"Bridge to armory, stand down weapons. Repeat, stand down."

Reed raised the phase pistol, and turned toward the console again.

That's when he saw that Alana was doing more than charging the weapons. She was targeting them on the Sarkassian ship.

"Stop!" he cried, loud enough this time that she heard him.

She turned, and saw him holding the phase pistol.

She picked up the pipe again, and headed straight for him.

Reed didn't have time to do anything other than react, and squeeze the trigger.

The blast caught her square in the stomach.

Her momentum carried her forward, and she crashed to the floor, the pipe clattering off toward one of the torpedo bays.

Her outstretched hand touched his, and their eyes met.

For an instant, he thought he saw the old Alana, thought he heard her speak to him.

Help.

And in that split-second, the wave of memories he had been experiencing all day overwhelmed him, became a flood, a whirlwind of moments flashing past in his mind.

He saw himself in the armory, on New Year's Eve, confronting Alana for an explanation of the Dinai incident, and then he was—

In her quarters, seeing the Corbett on her shelf, and then—

Back in the armory, standing an arm's length

away from her, and then they were kissing, and suddenly Reed was aware that he was seeing himself through her eyes, and that the memories he was reliving were not just his, they were Alana's too, that was the only explanation for what he was experiencing, though it was really no explanation at all as to why he should be reliving moments from her past. But he was, he was—

Standing at attention in the captain's ready room, listening to Archer's "Welcome aboard *Enterprise*" talk, and then he was—

On board the shuttlepod, heading for the Sarkassian outpost, and then—

Inside the pyramid, studying the tricorder intently, then—

Frozen in place, unable to move, back against one of the stones, and looming before him, eyes cold and unforgiving, a cruel smile twisting his face—

Goridian.

And then, everything went black.

Twenty-Three

HE WAS BACK IN THE PYRAMID.

Valay had the particle weapon in her right hand, and was pointing it directly at him. The phase pistol was in her left, held at her side. Kellan and Ash flanked her.

"Goodbye, Lieutenant Reed." The ambassador raised her weapon.

The sight of the gun pointing at him was like a splash of ice water in his face, forcing the past—and the memories that came with it—from his mind.

This was reality, Reed realized. His last few seconds of it, if he didn't do something.

"You want war?" he shouted suddenly. "Is that what you really want?"

He spoke to Valay, but the person he wanted to reach was Kellan.

"War?" The ambassador smiled. "Let it come. I suspect your forces are already preparing an offensive using the knowledge they gained from the commodore. In which case, our best course of action is an immediate attack."

Out of the corner of his eye, Reed saw Kellan step forward.

"War with Starfleet, Ambassador? We do not know how extensively their forces are spread throughout this region, nor how powerful their weapons are. Caution is advised."

"I know all about their weapons," Valay replied, not moving an inch. "*Enterprise* has phase cannons. *Enterprise* has photon torpedoes, *Enterprise* has plasma charges. None of which are a threat to a fully shielded Striker—much less two."

Reed was stunned into silence for a second. He tried to cover.

"You've left a few things out of our inventory, I'm afraid," he said, though Valay had, in fact, hit the nail right on the head when it came to listing their weapons. He wondered how.

"I don't think so," she said. "I think that covers everything."

He looked in her eyes and saw the certainty there.

So he turned to Kellan.

"We don't want a war. And from what I heard

you saying, it's not your first choice either. So trust your instincts, Kellan," Reed said. "Talk to your leaders—make sure Valay doesn't force your people down a road you don't want to take."

"Here and now, Ambassador Valay speaks for our leaders," he said. "She is their voice."

The words, for some reason, rang a bell with Reed. He didn't have time to figure out why, though.

"I would think that when it came to a matter of such importance, they'd want to speak for themselves—don't you? Funny how she won't let them, though."

Kellan looked puzzled. "What do you mean?"

"The jamming beam."

"The beam is there to prevent Roan from calling in others who may have been allied with him to betray our people."

"He's dead. Why do you need it now?"

Kellan's brow furrowed in thought.

"Call your government," Reed stepped forward, sensing he'd gotten through to him, at least a little bit. He locked eyes with the man. "Get instructions from them."

Valay stepped between the two of them.

"Very clever, Lieutenant," she said. "But I hardly think the colonel and I can be expected to forget that the jamming beam also prevents you from calling in your reinforcements as well."

"Our reinforcements?"

"The *Shi'ar*. Or have you forgotten about your rendezvous with her?"

This time, Reed didn't even bother to conceal his surprise.

"How on Earth . . . you *can't* know that."

She smiled. "I know things you can't imagine."

The way she said those words—he believed her.

His mind raced—there was no one he'd shared the information on the *Shi'ar* with, no way Valay could have accessed that data while she was on *Enterprise* unless she'd hacked into the most secure areas of their computer system, and he didn't think that was possible. But even assuming it was—that would have meant Ambassador Valay had planned this, or something like this even before she'd come aboard.

The thought made his head spin.

"We could partially disable the jamming beam, Ambassador," Kellan said hesitantly. "Give ourselves one of the lower frequencies to use, to contact the Council."

"Kellan," Valay said disapprovingly. "Think for a moment. Why would the lieutenant here want us to shut off the beam? Could it be that they have a device actively scanning the EM spectrum, looking for a way to break through and call reinforcements? Of course they do—which is why we cannot relax our guard for an instant."

"Yes, Ambassador," Kellan said. But he sounded skeptical. Reed couldn't blame him—Valay's reasoning sounded forced and faulty to him as well.

There was something very wrong going on here. Something that went beyond the civil war Reed thought he was caught in the middle of.

Kellan was still frowning.

Valay cast a sideways glance at him, and shifted.

"There may be a way to send a Relayer past the range of the jamming beam, Ambassador. Let me call the *Amileus* and—"

Valay spun and shot him with the phase pistol that was suddenly in her right hand.

Before the other man could react, she shot him as well.

Reed stumbled backward, trying to run, to lose himself among the stones. He bumped into one of them, still disoriented, and before he could right himself, Valay had the weapon targeted on him.

"Back out here, Lieutenant. Hands high, please."

He complied, taking a few slow steps forward.

"You seem set on a course of war, Ambassador," Reed said. "I wish I knew why."

"Let us just say that war suits my purposes, Lieutenant. The bloodier the better."

"Wasn't Dar Shalaan bloody enough for you? How many more Ta'alaat have to die—how many of your people, and mine?"

"That's close enough," she said. "We need to display your body prominently—right alongside

Kellan's here, I should think. That will do the trick."

She held the weapon in textbook-correct form—a surprise to Reed, since he didn't think firearms training was on the list of required courses in ambassadorial school.

But it shouldn't have been a surprise to him—not after everything else that had happened.

Not after seeing Valay change settings on the phase pistol, or hearing her reel off a list of *Enterprise*'s weapons, tell Kellan about their upcoming rendezvous with the *Shi'ar.*

And it wasn't just the things she knew that defied explanation. It was her actions—why she seemed so intent on forcing war between her people and the Ta'alaat, between her people and Starfleet. And she was going to succeed. There was nothing Reed could do to stop her. Nothing anyone could do—not Captain Archer, not any of the other Sarkassians. They would obey each and every one of her orders, without question. Just as Kellan had said.

"Here and now, Ambassador Valay speaks for our leaders. She is their voice."

And suddenly, Reed knew why those words had struck a chord with him.

He remembered Hoshi, reading from the Vulcan database—

"They spoke as our leaders, with the voice of our leaders, in the flesh of our leaders."

And Roan, telling him about the Anu'anshee—

"The technology involved—it often seems miraculous."

And Phlox, talking to him in sickbay—

"Some scientists believe that the essence of personality itself is contained within this field—what makes us individuals."

And his head cleared, just a little.

But it was enough.

Reed looked straight at Valay then, and recalled the words she'd spoken, about traitors, and reinforcements, and jamming beams, and realized they were all lies. It was all a role she was playing. The title, the robes, the words, the smile . . .

The body itself.

"Goridian," he said.

Light danced in her eyes, and she smiled.

Twenty-Four

GORIDIAN HERE, IN VALAY'S BODY.

Goridian aboard *Enterprise*, in Alana's.

Everything that a moment ago had been a whirl of confusion suddenly fell into place. Roan's murder, the attack in the brig, Alana's transformation—

"It wasn't amnesia," Reed said. "It wasn't her who tried to fire on the Sarkassians—it was you. You put your mind . . . inside her, somehow."

The words sounded ridiculous as he said them. The ambassador's smile twisted into a frown, and for a split second, he doubted his reasoning.

Then Valay smiled again, broader this time.

And Reed knew he was right.

He stepped forward, the uncertainty he'd felt a moment before now gone entirely. All that was left was a core of anger—burning bright inside him.

275

Valay raised her weapon.

"Stay right where you are, Lieutenant."

Reed forced himself to stop.

"Tell me how you did it. What you did to the ambassador—to Alana . . ."

"As you guessed. I took their places."

"But how?"

"The machines, of course. The Anu'anshee."

Reed didn't understand. "What machines?"

Valay took a step backward, still holding the phase pistol on him. And then she swiftly—expertly—switched weapons again, so that she was holding Kellan's in her right hand.

"Wouldn't do to shoot you with your own weapon, would it?" she said by way of explanation. "That would hardly prove compelling evidence of Earth's involvement in this affair to the Sarkassian Council."

Reed understood her plan now. His plan—he had to stop thinking of the person before him as Ambassador Valay. It was Goridian—and his goal was the same as it had been before, back aboard *Enterprise*.

"You want a war."

"That's right."

She raised the pistol again.

Valay, Goridian, whoever he thought of her as, she handled the gun like an expert. She stayed just far enough away from him that any attempt on his part to wrest it away from her would have failed.

"You're being foolish, Goridian. Stop and think for a second. War between Starfleet and the Sarkassians? That's not going to be some penny-ante struggle carried out with hand weapons and hidden explosives. It's going to be starship against starship. Thousand of people are likely to die. And do you know what? Bigger and better weapons are going to built—by us and the Sarkassians. Surely some of those will be used on your people."

"You forget who I am now, Lieutenant. I am a regent of the Empire. I will help direct the course of this war. Of course, my advice may seem puzzling at times to the Sarkassians, but they will understand my reasons—eventually." She smiled. "I suspect it will be a cathartic moment."

Reed's hand flexed unconsciously. He yearned for a weapon of his own—his phase pistol, or a knife, something, anything. He wanted Goridian to make a mistake, to come closer, for his attention to wander.

He needed more time to make something happen. "Tell me how the machines work," he said.

"I think not. We've wasted enough time as it is. I don't want any of the other Sarkassians coming to investigate—I'd have to shoot them as well, and the last thing I want to do is to have to explain another death. Three fatalities measured against yours and Roan's is believable—a very capable Starfleet officer, I will assure the Council. No stain upon the honor of the soldiers who died facing him. Any more, and the story will begin to strain the bonds of credulity."

She raised the particle weapon again.

"Goodbye, Lieutenant," she said. "I suspect your consciousness will not survive the next few seconds."

Her finger tightened on the trigger.

And then she paused, and lowered the gun.

"Your consciousness," she repeated, and a smile crossed her face. "I believe I will make a slight change in my plans."

She marched Reed over to one of the stones—the very one, it seemed to him, closest to where he'd first found Alana.

"What are you doing?" Reed asked.

"As I said, a slight change in plans. I've decided I will be far more useful to my government in the role of Lieutenant Malcolm Reed than Ambassador Valay Shuma." She smiled again. "You wanted to know how these worked? I'll show you."

Again making sure to stay just beyond his reach, keeping the particle weapon trained directly on him, she ran her free hand across the symbols covering the stone's surface in an apparently random order.

The stone began to glow, ever so slightly.

And before he could react, Reed felt himself snap backward, in the grip of some force he couldn't even began to comprehend, and slam up against the stone, his back stuck to it as if he'd been glued there.

He couldn't move. Not his feet, not his head, not his hands. He opened his mouth to speak, and found even that difficult.

"What the hell—"

"Consciousness transfer, Lieutenant," she said. "The Sarkassian scientists who found these stones thought they might have had other functions as well, but—I paid little attention to their speculations, to be honest. Once I realized how I could use these to infiltrate their empire."

Another piece of the puzzle clicked into place.

"You sent the distress call."

"That's right. I thought the Sarkassians would come charging in, Roan at the front of the pack. I set a trap for him. But instead"—she shrugged—"I caught your ensign."

The image he had seen earlier—Goridian appearing from behind one of the stones, and walking toward Alana—flashed through his mind again.

And suddenly he recalled an earlier memory.

And now he knew it for what it was.

The memory of what had happened when she had been surprised by Goridian. Held against the stone just as he was now.

But how was it that he could recall that moment? He hadn't been there, Alana had never said anything about it to him.

All at once, he felt the stone behind him growing warm.

The air, suddenly, smelled of electricity.

Valay took a step forward.

"I'd tell you this won't hurt," she said, "but I have no idea what it will feel like."

"Wait," Reed said. "What happens to me?"

"To you?"

"To my consciousness."

"Not my concern," she said. "Though from my reading of the scientists' notes, I expect that you die."

She reached out and touched his forehead, and the world went black.

Twenty-Five

MEMORIES RUSHED PAST, and rose up around him again.

His memories. And Alana's.

He was her, frozen in place, back pinned against the stone. Watching the alien walk toward her, hand outstretched. His fingertips brushed her brow—

And every inch of her being was suddenly on fire, screaming in agony.

The alien was there, inside her.

Two consciousnesses, two personalities, struggling for control of one body. The battle was furious, intense.

Alana lost the war, and went spinning off into the void.

* * *

Darkness surrounded her. She had no arms, no legs, no sense of sight, or smell, or touch, no way to communicate. It was like being in the isolation tank, back at the Academy. Part of their training for emergency evac conditions—no power, no lights, no way of telling whether or not time was passing. Totally disconnected from her environment—just like now.

But aware. And with that thought came the realization that she was alive.

Alive, and a prisoner. Trapped within her own body.

Time passed—how much, she had no way of knowing.

Occasionally, flashes of the world outside came through to her. The sound of a word, the smell of food, the ghosted image of a person, a room aboard *Enterprise*.

She could also—sometimes—sense the thoughts of the alien who had taken over her body. He was masquerading as her, taking her place among the crew.

The thought gave her renewed agony. But she couldn't do anything about it.

Helpless, she lost herself in the memories that were all she had left, and drifted away.

All at once, the world blossomed into light before her.

She was lying on the armory floor. Malcolm was on his hands and knees before her, staring at her in shock and confusion, his outstretched hand touching hers. Blood trickled down his forehead.

In that split second she was aware of two things:

The alien who had occupied her body was gone.

And she couldn't breathe.

She tried inhaling through her nose, then opening her mouth, and failed at both. Failed even to move a muscle, as if the electrical impulses from her brain were not reaching her limbs. As if there was a short-circuit somewhere.

The alien, she realized. He'd done something to her body.

She looked up at Malcolm. Help, she tried to say, and though her mouth didn't move, she could sense him, somehow, respond—as if his consciousness were somehow hearing her.

Their hands were touching.

She willed herself—

Into him.

A wave of memories overwhelmed her, moments the two of them had shared.

She saw herself in the armory, on New Year's Eve, as Malcolm confronted her for an explanation of the Dinai incident, and then they were—

In her quarters, as he pulled the Corbett from on her shelf, and turned to her with a smile on his face and they were—

Back in the armory, standing an arm's length apart, and then they were kissing, and suddenly she was aware that she was seeing herself through his eyes, and that the memories she was reliving were not just hers, they were his too, that the two of them were together.

Two consciousnesses, sharing one body.

His in control, still—but hers there. Drifting on the edge of his awareness.

Hesitantly at first, and then with more urgency, she began to try to communicate with him.

Reed could hear her clearly now.

And as he listened, the last piece of the puzzle fell into place.

The hallucinatory intensity of his memories, why he'd been so preoccupied with the past these last few days—why every place he turned, everywhere he looked, seemed to remind him of Alana.

She had been with him this whole time, ever since they'd touched back in the armory.

Alana was alive.

He felt himself—his consciousness—reach out for hers, and . . .

They stood facing each other, on a flat, featureless plain that seemed to stretch out to eternity in all directions.

"It's you," Reed said hesitantly, taking a step forward. "My God, it's really you."

Her next words were like ice water on his face.

"No," she said. "It's not me at all. None of this"—she waved her hands around—"is real."

Of course she was right, Reed realized instantly. This was an illusion, created in their heads. His head. A meeting of the minds.

"That's right," she said. "Reality is out there—Goridian, a split second away from touching you. From invading your body, and taking control."

"We'll stop him—together," Reed said. "Two against one."

She shook her head. "No. He's too strong."

"Then how—"

He read her thoughts then, and his heart sank.

"No," he said, and then louder, "No!"

"It's the only way, Malcolm." She smiled sadly, and took a step back.

He reached out for her, and the plain around them vanished.

"Remember me."

Her consciousness brushed against his, then.

A last, parting touch—the echo of a kiss.

Light flooded his senses, and the world returned.

He was back in the pyramid. No time had passed.

Valay's hand was still pressed against his forehead. She still wore the same smile.

Then she screamed in agony, and fell to the ground. Seizing just the way Alana had, what seemed like ages ago, when he'd first come across her on the planet's surface.

Reed knew now what those seizures had represented—Goridian struggling for control of her body. Just the way these seizures represented Alana—her consciousness, struggling to keep Goridian from leaving Valay's body, and taking control of Reed.

Somehow—Anu'anshee technology, of course, though the details were beyond him—once Goridian had used the machine, his consciousness was free to wander at will. That was how he'd gotten back to his own body after Alana's "death" in the armory, how he'd taken over Valay in the cell. He didn't really need the machines at all anymore, had probably just intended to use it to keep Reed immobile long enough to transfer into his body.

But what was true for Goridian was true for Alana as well now. She could jump from body to body at will, as she had when she and Reed touched back in sickbay.

Reed felt the force holding him to the stone loosen, and he struggled free of it.

He bent down and picked up the particle weapon from the ground.

Valay—Valay's body—was still seizing. The two minds—Alana's and Goridian's—struggling for control. Reed reached for the ambassador, intending to do something, what he wasn't sure, but he couldn't let Alana fight alone against—

The seizures stopped, and Valay lay on the ground a moment, not moving.

Then she rose to her feet.

Hoping against hope, Reed looked in her eyes.

They were pinpricks of black. Cold, and unfeeling.

Goridian.

He raised the particle weapon.

"You can't," Valay—Goridian—said. "She's still in here, you know. Alive."

"I know," Reed said. Alana had known too—what would happen. What he would have to do.

"Good-bye," he said. "That's for her, you bastard. Not you."

Valay's mouth opened in surprise.

Reed gritted his teeth, and fired.

The security stopped, and Vater Ror on the
round a formation moving

Then he rose to a halt.

Holographic name Read floated in her eyes.
They were unpacked or Mack Gold and the
richer

Gorman.

He raised the portable weapon

You can, Vater—Gorman—said, "Not well
to bear you locate alive."

"I regret," Read said, while had mount co—
what would happen. What I would have to do
to show," he said. Start venting, you bet
said her you.

Vater moved forward in surprise.

Read raised his torch and fired.

Epilogue

"MESSAGE BEGINS. Captain Jonathan Archer of the *Starship Enterprise* to Nicole and Jonathan Hart, Lake Armstrong, Luna. Mr. and Ms. Hart, by now you've received notification from Starfleet about your daughter's death. I want you to know you have my condolences, and the condolences of everyone aboard this ship who served with Alana. She was a special person, and she will be missed. And I can tell you that what she did will not be forgotten—her actions helped prevent a war that could have cost untold lives."

Archer steepled his hands together on the desk in front of him, and took a breath. No uncertainty about what to say this time—though Archer thought it best to leave the circumstances of Hart's passing deliberately vague. Not because he doubted what had happened, but because to anyone who hadn't been here, hadn't seen the strange events of the last few days unfold before their own eyes, it all sounded more than a little preposterous. Supernatural, perhaps.

He finished his message to the Harts by telling them to expect other communiqués from the crew to follow—Malcolm, he knew, was planning on passing on their daughter's effects with a note of his own. There would be something else in there as well for the Harts to hold on to.

As if that could ever replace what they'd lost.

The door chime sounded.

"Come."

Trip walked in. "You get that message done?"

"Yes, I did. In fact—" Archer punched a button on the workstation, and smiled. "I just sent it."

"Good." Trip nodded. "Thought I'd come by and pick you up for the funeral. Everybody's heading down there already."

"Malcolm too?"

"Uh-huh."

"How's he doing?"

"Holding up pretty good, I'd say—all things considered. I think you did the right thing, Captain. Letting him give the eulogy."

"I'm glad." Archer thought again about asking Trip how much truth there was to the rumors regarding Reed and Hart's relationship. The ship's grapevine reached up to the ready room just as well as anywhere else on the ship, but Archer never put much trust in the rumors he heard that way. He depended on people that he trusted to verify that information. But in this instance, he doubted that Trip would tell him much—even if he did know more than Archer.

Not that any of it mattered now, not at this point.

Unfortunate.

It was a stupid regulation anyway. He added it to the growing list of things he looked forward to discussing with Admiral Forrest.

The com sounded.

"Captain." It was Hoshi. "Transmission coming in—from the Sarkassians."

He and Trip glanced at each other.

"On my way," Archer said, and hurried onto the bridge.

They'd had no word from the Sarkassians since Reed had returned from the planet's surface yesterday. They'd tracked a flurry of com traffic between the Sarkassian ships—and a few hours afterward, the jamming beam had gone down, and there was even more subspace traffic, between the ships and the Sarkassian Council, no doubt.

"Put it up," he said, nodding to the screen.

The monitor filled with the image of another Sarkassian, one Archer didn't recognize at all. Significantly younger than either Roan or Valay had been.

"*Enterprise,* this is Lieutenant Col of the *Striker Amileus.*"

"Lieutenant."

"We have found the records from our outpost. The story your lieutenant put forth—regarding Commodore Roan and the ambassador—it appears to be possible."

"Well." Archer smiled. "I'm glad to hear you say that."

"Even so," Col's face remained grim, "I am authorized to inform you that your actions in interfering with our affairs—and in removing Sarkassian property from the outpost—are cause for great concern."

"Seems to me we helped you set your affairs in order," Archer said. "And saved a lot of lives in the process."

It seemed to him as well that a little "thank you" might be in order, but he suspected that was not on the list of items Col wanted to discuss with him.

"As for your property," Archer continued, "we returned that. As I think you know."

"We retrieved the sample containers from the outpost's surface. However, I have been instructed to inform you that your possession of any artifacts or records of such artifacts would be considered tantamount to an act of war. Which would be responded to in kind."

"We understand," Archer said. "And as our lieutenant told you—we've returned everything that we took from the outpost."

"And the records?"

Archer sighed. "If you insist—we will destroy them."

"We insist," Col said.

"Very well." He'd expected this—had already asked Hoshi and Malcolm to gather together their data in a single node on the network, so it would be easier to wipe clean. He'd already talked himself out of keeping a second copy of the data hidden elsewhere in the system.

When the Sarkassians were ready to deal with the rest of the galaxy in a more open manner, that information would be available again. He wasn't going to lecture them on the importance of being good neighbors, though.

That, he was saving for T'Pol.

"We'll have every record from the outpost wiped from the system in a matter of minutes."

"Good. I will take your word for this."

Archer nodded. "Good."

"Then I believe our business here is finished, *Enterprise*. You are free to leave our space."

"And don't let the door hit you on the way out," Trip added quietly, from behind the captain.

"One last thing, Col. We answered the distress call because we wanted to help. Remember that. And if you want help in the future—we'll be around."

Col seemed momentarily taken aback by Archer's statement.

And at that moment, T'Pol stepped forward.

Archer glanced sideways at his science officer, and suppressed a small smile.

In the long-distant past, the Vulcans had been a volatile, destructive people. Having served with T'Pol for over a year now, he knew that those emotions, suppressed though they were by the discipline of logic she practiced, were still present, buried deep beneath her calm exterior.

Once in a while, though, he caught a hint of them. Most recently, in the ready room, when T'Pol had told him the gist of what she was going to say to the Sarkassians.

Archer settled back in his chair.

This ought to be good, he thought.

"Lieutenant Col, I stand here as both a member of Starfleet, and a representative of the planet Vulcan. It is in that latter capacity that I speak now.

"I must be blunt, Lieutenant. You and your scientists have behaved irresponsibly. You are like children given a box of dangerous weapons. You take them out and play with them, one by one, not knowing or caring what damage you do to others or yourself. Your dangerous activities threaten to harm not only yourselves, but others. On behalf of my government, I urge you to cease your careless exploitation of the resources left by the Anu'anshee."

Archer watched Col throughout the speech by T'Pol. The lieutenant's expressionless mask gradually gave way to an expression of anger.

"Who are you to lecture us?"

"That was not a lecture, merely a statement of fact," T'Pol said. "In two days we rendezvous with the Vulcan research vessel *Shi'ar.* She will carry information back to Vulcan regarding the nature and kind of your activities."

"Meaning what?"

"Meaning the matter is now out of our hands, I suppose," Archer said. "How you eventually decide to relate to the rest of the galaxy is up to you."

He looked at Col. The man still stood, ramrod straight, on the bridge of his ship. He hadn't moved an inch.

In his eyes, though, Archer thought he saw some give. Or maybe it was only wishful thinking on his part.

Someday, he hoped to find out for sure.

"Goodbye, Lieutenant," Archer said. "And good luck."

At his nod, Hoshi closed the circuit.

"Excuse me—if we could get started."

From the back of the armory—jammed in among the rest of the crew, who filled the small room to overflowing, crowding in on the ladders, on the second-floor gantry, along the two torpedo bays—Archer craned his neck and watched Lieutenant Reed, at the firing console, as he waved his hands for attention.

The room quickly fell silent.

"Thank you," Reed said. "I have a certain reputation to uphold here—as a man of few words—and I promise not to disappoint."

Archer smiled.

Reed cleared his throat, and clasped his hands behind his back.

"We're gathered here today to pay our respects to our fallen comrade. Ensign Alana Hart—who, I think I speak for all of us in saying, we never got to know quite as well as we should have." Reed cut the last word short, and stood quite still for a moment.

Archer suddenly realized how hard this was for Malcolm—and suspected that there was more than a little truth to the rumors he'd heard.

He swallowed hard himself then, and exhaled deeply.

"We honor her and remember her by being here," Reed continued, "and I think Alana would also agree that we honor her by continuing to look forward, toward the future, and not to focus too hard on the past."

He nodded then, and the members of the armory crew—Bishop, Diaz, Santini, and Perkins, who'd just rotated in, stepped forward and saluted him crisply. Reed returned the salute.

Archer's eyes, and the eyes of all those around

him, of everyone crowded into the armory, turned then toward the starboard torpedo bay, where Alana's body lay inside an empty tube—a makeshift coffin.

At the firing console, Reed was mouthing something quietly to himself. Good-bye? A prayer? Archer didn't know.

The lieutenant reached down and pressed a button on the console.

The torpedo tube slid along the bay, and into the firing chamber. The airlock sealed shut behind it. A second later, Archer heard the sound of the tube being shot off into space.

"Godspeed, Ensign," the captain whispered.

He turned back and saw Reed, still at the console, facing away from the crew, his shoulders shaking ever so slightly.

Reed did not turn around for a long time.

The crew dispersed. Archer made his way to the firing console, where Reed was talking to the rest of the armory crew.

"Nicely done, Malcolm," the captain said. "I feel sure that she's watching us and smiling from somewhere."

"Thank you, sir. I hope so."

Archer joined in their discussion—a gentle razzing of Perkins, the newcomer. A gentle razzing of Reed's leadership style. A few memories of Ensign Hart.

The com sounded.

"T'Pol to Captain Archer."

"Go ahead, Sub-Commander."

"We are approaching another star system."

"Already?"

"I had put us at warp four to make our scheduled appointment with the *Shi'ar*."

"Right. So what about this star?"

"Data coming in now . . . two Minshara-class planets, in synchronous orbit about the star."

"Synchronous orbit?" Archer frowned. "What's that mean?"

"One hundred eighty degrees opposite each other sir, along the orbital plane. The planets also appear to be . . . mirror images of one another."

She sounded puzzled. Archer was too.

"I'll be right there. Out."

He turned to Reed, who was frowning as well.

"Mirror images, a hundred and eighty degrees apart along the orbital path—how is that possible?"

Reed shook his head. "It's not, sir. At least, not in my experience."

"Well. Come on, then, Malcolm." Archer walked over to the armory door, which hissed open at his approach. "Let's go broaden your experience."

Reed smiled then—the first genuine smile the captain had seen from him in days—and moved toward the open door.

ACKNOWLEDGMENTS

A lot of people helped make this book happen in a timely fashion, though I must single out in particular:

Margaret Clark, who has a calm demeanor . . .
Paula Block, who has good questions . . .
The Pocket Rocket, the real D.O., the one and only managing editor who can take a licking (or at least, an airplane-spinning) and keep on ticking . . .
And of course, the family—Caleb, Cleo, Jill, Madeleine, and Toni.

Thanks are also due to:

The Pocket Books production staff.
Vonda McIntyre, for a most opportune shot of inspiration.
Mike Okuda, who provided valuable technical

info and once, long ago, in a galaxy far, far away, let me sit in the captain's chair.

Rick Berman and Brannon Braga, who created *Enterprise*, and thus brought forth manna from heaven.

And Gene Roddenberry, without whom . . .

Coming in March 2003

Surak's Soul

by J. M. Dillard

Captain's Starlog. Supplemental. While mapping an area of uncharted space, we have encountered a populated planet—which is sending out a beacon that our universal translator has garbled. Hoshi is currently trying to decipher what she can.

Jonathan Archer sat in his command chair on the bridge of the *Enterprise* and stared at the image of the M-class planet on the main viewscreen before him: the larger-than-Earth globe, blue-speckled with large verdant islands rather than continents, rotated lazily.

Frankly, Archer was grateful for the signal, and suspected the rest of his crew was, as well; the process of mapping lifeless planet after lifeless planet had grown tedious, and he was looking forward to some interspecies interaction. He was hoping that this particular planet, which they would have labeled Kappa Xi II, was transmitting its signal in order to welcome interstellar travelers.

But, as he turned to look expectantly at Hoshi (already under the scrutiny of Travis Mayweather at helm, Malcolm Reed at tactical, and T'Pol at the science station), his hope grew fainter. As Hoshi listened and relistened to the message, her dark eyes focused on a far-distant point, her lips resolved themselves into a thinner and thinner line, and the crease between her delicate jet brows deepened.

"Anything?" Archer prompted at last.

"I need more time to do a thorough translation." Hoshi shook her head, then added, "It's not good."

"How so?"

"I'm pretty sure it's a distress call. Some sort of medical emergency. But I can't get any more detailed than that. . . ." She sighed. "From the articulation of the sounds, I'd say the population is humanoid; at least, their lips and tongues and teeth are like ours."

Archer considered this for no more than a matter of seconds, then turned to T'Pol. "What's the atmosphere down there?"

The Vulcan swiveled elegantly to her station, then looked back at the captain, her expression and tone impassive, despite the news she conveyed. "Breathable. However . . ." Her gaze became pointed. "I detect very few life-forms."

It took Archer no more than an instant to make a decision. Regardless of the number of survivors, *Enterprise* was present, capable of assistance, and therefore obligated to intervene. An entire species, perhaps, was at risk of annihilation. He pressed the intercom. "Archer to sickbay."

"Phlox here."

Keeping his gaze fixed on the worried Hoshi, Archer said, "Doctor, we have an unknown medical emergency down on the planet's surface; the population is probably humanoid. Bring whatever you need to the shuttlepod launch bay. Archer out."

He stood. "Hoshi, I'll need you to translate what you can. T'Pol . . ." He gestured with his chin, and together the three of them headed for the bridge doors. "Mister Mayweather, you have the conn."

The flight down to Kappa Xi II's surface was pleasant; Archer was privately cheered by Hoshi's attitude toward it. She had made up her mind to learn to enjoy such expeditions, and peered through the small viewscreen at the looming image of large emerald islands adrift in a vast turquoise sea—a far different distribution of land to water than Earth's.

"Gorgeous," Archer murmured, half to himself, as he piloted the shuttlepod closer to one of the larger islands, their destination.

"Yes," Hoshi echoed, while Phlox made an enthusiastic noise. "Too bad they're having an emergency. This looks like it would be a beautiful place for shore leave . . ."

"It *is* rather Earth-like," T'Pol commented neutrally from the copilot's chair, which made the captain consider that a blue-green planet might seem inviting to humans from what he'd heard, but perhaps to Vulcan eyes, a red desert planet would be more aesthetically pleasing.

Still, the ride down through the atmosphere to the coastline of the island was breathtaking; the water closer to the shore was celery-colored and so clear that even from a distance, brightly colored creatures could be seen swimming beneath the surface. The sand was pure white, reminding Archer of a Florida beach he'd once visited; at the meeting of water and shore, long-legged birds raced to pluck buried meals from the wet sand before waves rolled in again.

Archer brought the shuttlepod to a smooth landing at its destination, a large paved strip closest to the largest cluster of remaining life-forms. He had wondered whether this large paved area was used strictly for airflight—but a glance at his surroundings made it clear that this culture, if not used to extraterrestrial contact, was probably capable of spaceflight. In a nearby hangar, a number of sophisticated and apparently spaceworthy vessels rested; Archer eyed them covetously as he brought the shuttlepod to a halt, wishing there were time to inspect them. Instead, he pushed the hatch controls open, and followed his away team out onto the landing strip, adjacent to the coastline.

Once he was outside, the first thing Archer noticed was the sun. Shining bright in a cloudless Earth-blue sky, it reflected off the nearby diamond-white sand, off the dappled water, off tall, spiraling buildings that shone like mother-of-pearl, reflecting pale green, turquoise, and rose. Tall trees, their great blue-green leaves draping down like weeping willows, rustled in a light breeze.

"An island paradise." Archer sighed. Trip would have felt at home down here, given the time he'd spent in the Keys. The landing party had dressed in the large—and rather unwieldy, the captain thought—space suits on Phlox's insistence. Had the captain been alone, he would have risked exposure and relied on the decontam procedures on board the *Enterprise* just for the chance to feel the sun and wind against his bare skin. The notion of breathing in a lungful of sea air was enticing. Besides, the suits, with their great domed headgear, might make them look rather outlandish to any species unused to regular extraterrestrial contact. But he respected Phlox's opinion, and where his crew members were concerned, he would take all precautions. Reed had insisted on their arming themselves with phase pistols. Medical emergency or not, it was impossible to predict exactly what they might encounter.

"Ambient temperature twenty-five degrees Celsius," T'Pol announced clinically, her gaze on her scanner. "Life-forms . . ." She paused, then pointed in the direction of the spiraling buildings. "In that direction, Captain. Very few, and very faint."

"Let's move," Archer said, all appreciation for his surroundings dismissed. He led the group at a rapid pace, slowing only when Hoshi cried out behind him.

"Captain!"

He turned and followed his communication officer's gaze. Peeking out from the profile of one of the silver ships was a hand. Not a human hand—this one was six-fingered, curled in a limp half fist, the skin a deep greenish bronze.

Archer arrived at the humanoid's side first, closely followed by Phlox. In the open hatch of the shuttle-sized ship, a male had fallen backward, so that his torso lay faceup on the stone-and-shale landing strip, his legs on the deck of his vessel. Clearly, he'd been stricken as he attempted to leave . . . fleeing, perhaps, whatever had decimated his people. His complexion was deep bronze, his scalp and ridged brow entirely hairless; the cartilage of his nose terminated in a sharp, triangular tip, framed by large diagonal slits for nostrils. He stared up at the cloudless sky with almost perfectly round, dark eyes, dulled by death. His expression was entirely neutral, his lipless mouth open to reveal a hard dental ridge mostly covered by pale gums. The hands that fell so limply from his flailed arms were slightly webbed, suggesting that his people had evolved from the sea that covered most of their planet.

Whatever had taken his life, Archer decided, had not inspired fear in him, even if he was running away. He got the impression that the man had sagged gently to the ground, as if he had simply no longer been able to hold himself erect.

Phlox crouched over the body and scanned it briefly. He glanced up at Archer and said softly, sadly, "Already dead, I fear. Very recently."

Archer gave a single regretful nod.

The doctor studied his readouts, then gently touched the dead humanoid, examining the eyes, nose, mouth, and torso. "I'm not detecting anything microbial in his system . . ." He looked up at Archer, his features furrowed with puzzlement. "In fact, I can't really tell you what he died of. My first guess is that these readings are normal for him . . . but it would help if I had a healthy member of his race for comparison."

"Captain," T'Pol said quietly. Archer took a step toward her and glanced over her shoulder at her scanner. "Chances of finding such a being are becoming slimmer. Since we have left *Enterprise*, many more life-forms have died. I'm now reading only eleven on this island. The signals are growing increasingly faint."

"Let's move," Archer said again, gazing down at

the dead man, feeling oddly reluctant to leave him without some acknowledgment, some rite to mark his passage. But as the captain turned to face the alien city, he realized the necessity for speed—else they would be needing a memorial to mark the passage of an entire civilization.

As the quartet strode quickly over a shale-and-sand street toward the building T'Pol indicated, they were met by grisly sights: pedestrians fallen as they walked, in different stages of decomposition under the bright sun. Airborne vehicles carrying single passengers, sometimes pairs, had dropped from the sky, leaving mangled wreckage and corpses—some on the ground, others caught in the swaying trees, or on shrubs, or lying atop a bier of brightly colored flowers. At one point, they passed a body being attended to by a carrion bird; Hoshi briefly closed her eyes, but moved stalwartly onward. Once again, Archer got the impression that the victims had surrendered easily and unexpectedly to death, in the midst of going about their lives.

He was finally glad for the awkward suit, with its self-contained atmosphere; the smell of decay must have been overwhelming. He thought of Earth's past plagues, and the terror that must have been felt by the survivors. During the Black Plague in medieval Europe, there had been so many dead, the living could not bury them all; a similar thing had happened during the plagues that swept mankind after the Third World War. And it had happened to these poor people, in the midst of their beautiful paradise.

He maintained silence, forcing himself to concentrate on the waiting survivors who needed their help; only Hoshi spoke, uttering a single plaintive remark.

"I only hope there's someone left for me to try to talk to."

No one replied—not even Phlox. The streets were still, quiet save for the sound of wind rustling through long leaves, and the cries of seabirds.

The landing party soon reached their destination: a building with shimmering, nacreous walls that coiled delicately skyward, its shape reminding Archer of a nautilus shell. Large windows overlooked the sea.

Yet the building's beauty belied the horror that waited inside: as Archer and his group entered, they were met by an eerie sight. In a large sun-filled room with a view of the sparkling beach, some sixty or seventy bronze-skinned people sat cross-legged on the padded floor—some fallen forward, faces pressed to the ground, others fallen back against the walls. The room was crowded beyond its capacity, so that late arrivals knelt in the room's center, pressed so tightly against their neighbors that even in death, they were held upright. All wore the same gentle, relaxed expression of the first casualty the away team had encountered.

Hoshi failed to entirely suppress a gasp; even T'Pol's eyes, behind her visor, flickered for an instant as she steadied herself to do a quick scan.

"Survivors this way," she said softly, pointing down a gleaming corridor.

Phlox turned his broad body directly toward the sight, absorbing it fully. "A shame," he said. "A peaceful people, able to build such a marvelous city . . . And now, most of them gone."

Archer put a hand on his shoulder. "Let's go find those survivors, Doctor."

Phlox turned, shaking his head as he moved alongside the captain. "You read of such things happening in history, but you never wish to see such a thing yourself. . . ."

T'Pol led the way down the corridor; they passed several rooms, all of them filled with exotic-looking beds made of a shimmering gelatinous material that caught Archer's eye, but there was no time left to stop and inspect them. Atop each one lay one, sometimes two, bodies; after a time, Archer stopped looking.

A moment or two later, the Vulcan said, with the faintest hint of something suspiciously akin to excitement, "Survivor, Captain. This room. . . ."

They entered; Archer moved aside so Phlox could attend to his patient at once. Eagerly, Hoshi moved beside the doctor, in case she was needed to communicate. The alien—this one, judging by her more delicate features and smaller size, female—was partially encased in a bed composed of a blue-green gelatinous substance suspended in the air.

Phlox scanned the woman, then exchanged a knowing glance with T'Pol.

"What?" Archer demanded of the two.

Both paused, then Phlox spoke. "This woman has just died."

"Another survivor," T'Pol added swiftly. "Approximately zero-point-one-seven kilometers down the corridor. . . ."

Archer made his way into the hallway at a speed just shy of a full run; T'Pol outpaced him, leading the way as Hoshi and Phlox followed. Two doors down, the Vulcan entered what appeared to be a large, fully-equipped medical laboratory. Several suspended beds lay empty, but on the one nearest the entrance lay a patient—half covered by the body of another alien, who had apparently been standing over the bed when he was stricken.

The bed itself was glowing, phosphorescent, slightly pulsating; Archer could feel the warmth it emanated as he helped T'Pol lift the body of the male off the prone patient.

As the *Enterprise* officers gently eased the male to the floor, Phlox leaned forward and ran a scanner over his chest. "Dead." The doctor turned and swiftly made his way over to the reclining patient—a female. "But she's alive!" His tone was one of pure triumph; as he ran his medical scanner over her, he reported, "But weakening with each second. Electrolyte readings differ from those found in the dead victims. . . ." He opened his medical case and prepared an injection. As he administered it, the blue-green bed flickered, then began to brighten, shot through with glowing phosphorescent veins.

"A nutrient bed," Phlox murmured, while he attended the woman. "Probably to counteract the weakness. I'll wager it's to help stabilize her electrolytes. . . ." He trailed off, absorbed in his work.

Archer, meantime, could not help noticing the expression on the male victim's face; of all the dead the captain had seen, only this man's countenance was not peaceful. Indeed, his features were contorted with what a human would call outrage, even—*Am I reading my own cultural cues into this?* Archer wondered—recognition, as if he had recognized the cause of his own death and been incensed by it.

"Anyone else still with us?" Archer asked softly of T'Pol, who was busily scanning for readings.

Her eyes narrowed. "No survivors in this building. But roughly point-five-four kilometers northeast, there's one fairly strong signal left."

"And the others?"

Her gaze grew pointed. "There *are* no others, Captain. Not on this island. Not anymore."

You had said there were eleven, Archer almost said, then realized the futility of challenging the accuracy of T'Pol's reading. In the moments since they'd arrived on the island, nine of those survivors had died.

He made a decision. "Stay with her," he told Phlox, who was busily bent over the surviving female. "Hoshi, you come with us. T'Pol and I are going to go find the last survivor and bring him back here; we might need your help communicating after all."

"Fascinating medical apparata," Phlox murmured, his gaze fixed on his patient, but Hoshi nodded in acknowledgment.

"Aye, sir."

Despite the fact that they were in the midst of a city, T'Pol led the captain and Hoshi into what seemed to be a livestock facility, where smooth-skinned quadrupeds, looking rather like overfed manatees on legs, lay motionless, perished in their separate stalls. Troughs of untouched grain and water lay in each pen. Overhead were storage lofts holding containers of what appeared to be feed.

There was an endearing ugliness about the creatures, and the fact that the pens were clean and in fact padded for comfort made Archer somehow sadder than he'd been before. It was hard enough to witness the death of a sentient being, who was aware of his own mortality; but there was a special poignancy about the demise of a less intelligent creature who trusted others for its care. The image of his beagle, Porthos, flashed in Archer's mind.

A single glance at Hoshi's heartbroken expression made Archer look away.

"All recently deceased," T'Pol said clinically, passing them with no more than a cursory glance.

Archer hardened his attitude and followed the Vulcan closely, focusing on the task at hand. "So the plague—or whatever's caused this—has affected their animals, too."

"With the exception of some of their avian fauna," T'Pol remarked—then came to an abrupt halt, lifting a hand for silence.

Archer stopped behind her; Hoshi, third in line, bumped into him.

The two women heard the noise first—of course, given T'Pol's acute Vulcan hearing and Hoshi's amazing exolinguistic ears. Both looked upward—expectantly—at the same area in one of the lofts.

Hoshi uttered a few tentative sounds in the aliens' tongue, her voice a little higher-pitched than normal—whether from proper pronunciation or fear, Archer could not tell. A greeting, perhaps, or an offer to help.

What happened next happened so quickly that for Archer, it all blurred together.

An alien face—deep bronze, with round, luminous, *living* eyes, appeared overhead amid the stacks of feed containers. A male, given his size and bulk; the low-ceilinged loft forced him to crawl on hands and knees. He scrambled to the edge of the loft and looked down at the landing party.

Glowered, actually, but Archer's observation was overwhelmed by the jubilant thought: *Alive! He's alive and strong enough to talk!*

And, indeed, the alien opened his lipless mouth and let go a sound. An unarticulated sound, more like a low growl that began deep in his broad chest and left his throat as a shriek . . .

. . . As he came springing down, arms outstretched, one webbed, many-fingered hand grasping, its target Hoshi's throat.

The communications officer screamed as the alien leapt atop her, knocking her down hard—so hard that, despite the size of the helmet, Archer could hear her skull thud.

Weakened or not, the alien produced a small object—a utility knife, Archer thought—and lifted it upward with the clear intent of bring it down in the vicinity of Hoshi's neck.

Archer had no way of knowing whether the knife could pierce the strong fiber of Hoshi's suit, of knowing whether the alien could do her any serious harm. He responded out of pure instinct—drawing the phase pistol, putting his gloved finger on the trigger, aiming and preparing to fire.

But before he could do so, another's phase blast, painfully precise, caught and illumined the alien in the instant before he could bring down the blade.

He shuddered, hesitated in the air a half second, then fell heavily to one side, allowing the terrified Hoshi to scrabble backward, crablike, on her arms and legs.

Archer reached Hoshi's side first; she grimaced and rubbed the back of her skull—in vain, since her suit kept her from any hands-on contact with the injured area. "I'm fine," she told the captain ruefully. "I tried to say that we were here to help, but the alien . . . He didn't seem sane."

The two humans glanced over at the fallen man, and at T'Pol, who bent over him with her tricorder. Her pistol was already reholstered, her air already that of the impassive scientist; yet there was the subtlest catch in her tone as she looked up at Archer and announced:

"Dead, Captain. Given his weakened state, my stun blast killed him."

Look for STAR TREK fiction from Pocket Books

Star Trek®

Star Trek: Deep Space Nine®

Novelizations

Enterprise®

Star Trek®: New Frontier

Star Trek®: Stargazer

Star Trek®: Starfleet Corps of Engineers (eBooks)

Star Trek®: Invasion!

#1 • *First Strike* • Diane Carey
#2 • *The Soldiers of Fear* • Dean Wesley Smith & Kristine Kathryn Rusch
#3 • *Time's Enemy* • L.A. Graf
#4 • *The Final Fury* • Dafydd ab Hugh
Invasion! Omnibus • various

Star Trek®: Day of Honor

#1 • *Ancient Blood* • Diane Carey
#2 • *Armageddon Sky* • L.A. Graf
#3 • *Her Klingon Soul* • Michael Jan Friedman
#4 • *Treaty's Law* • Dean Wesley Smith & Kristine Kathryn Rusch
The Television Episode • Michael Jan Friedman
Day of Honor Omnibus • various

Star Trek®: The Captain's Table

#1 • *War Dragons* • L.A. Graf
#2 • *Dujonian's Hoard* • Michael Jan Friedman
#3 • *The Mist* • Dean Wesley Smith & Kristine Kathryn Rusch
#4 • *Fire Ship* • Diane Carey
#5 • *Once Burned* • Peter David
#6 • *Where Sea Meets Sky* • Jerry Oltion
The Captain's Table Omnibus • various

Star Trek®: The Dominion War

#1 • *Behind Enemy Lines* • John Vornholt
#2 • *Call to Arms...* • Diane Carey
#3 • *Tunnel Through the Stars* • John Vornholt
#4 • *...Sacrifice of Angels* • Diane Carey

Star Trek®: Section 31™

Rogue • Andy Mangels & Michael A. Martin
Shadow • Dean Wesley Smith & Kristine Kathryn Rusch
Cloak • S.D. Perry
Abyss • David Weddle & Jeffrey Lang

Star Trek®: Gateways

#1 • *One Small Step* • Susan Wright
#2 • *Chainmail* • Diane Carey
#3 • *Doors Into Chaos* • Robert Greenberger
#4 • *Demons of Air and Darkness* • Keith R.A. DeCandido